THE LADY GRACE MYSTERIES

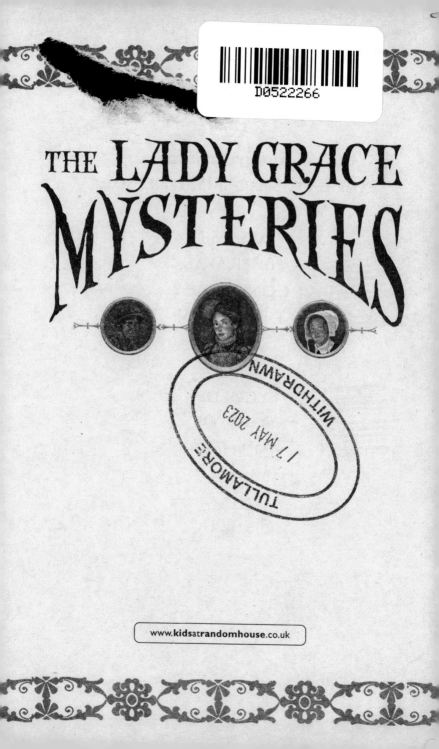

www.kidsatrandomhouse.co.uk

Also available in
THE LADY GRACE MYSTERIES series

❋

THE LADY GRACE MYSTERIES

LOOT

Grace Cavendish

Jan Burchett and Sara Vogler are writing as Grace Cavendish

RED FOX

THE LADY GRACE MYSTERIES: LOOT
A RED FOX BOOK 978 1 862 30420 8

First published in Great Britain by Red Fox,
an imprint of Random House Children's Books
A Random House Group Company

This edition published 2010

1 3 5 7 9 10 8 6 4 2

Series created by Working Partners Ltd
Copyright © Working Partners Ltd, 2010
Cover illustration by David Wyatt

The Random House Group Limited supports the Forest Stewardship Council (FSC), the leading
international forest certification organization. All our titles that are printed on Greenpeace-approved
FSC-certified paper carry the FSC logo. Our paper procurement policy can be found at
www.rbooks.co.uk/environment.

Set in Bembo by
Falcon Oast Graphic Art Ltd.

Red Fox Books are published by Random House Children's Books,
61–63 Uxbridge Road, London W5 5SA

www.kidsatrandomhouse.co.uk
www.rbooks.co.uk

Addresses for companies within The Random House Group Limited can be found at:
www.randomhouse.co.uk/offices.htm

THE RANDOM HOUSE GROUP Limited Reg. No. 954009

A CIP catalogue record for this book is available from the British Library.

Printed and bound in Great Britain by
CPI Bookmarque, Croydon, CR0 4TD

For Sara and Jennifer Burgess,
and in memory of my
dear friend Carol.

Love from Jan

Most Privy and Secrete

The daybooke of my Lady Grace Cavendish,
Maid of Honour to Her Glorious Majesty
Queen Elizabeth I of that name

At the Palace of Placentia,
Greenwich, England

Evil Be to Any Who Look Herein

The Fourteenth Day of January, in the Year of
Our Lord 1571

The Palace of Placentia, Greenwich
My bedchamber, almost nine of the clock

Here I am, squashed into a corner of my
bedchamber, far from the fire, while Mary Shelton
and Lady Sarah Bartelmy fuss about new gowns
that the Maids have all been gifted. Well, *Sarah* is
fussing – as usual – and Mary is trying to pacify
her. Sometimes I think it is tiresome to share a
bedchamber with two other Maids of Honour –
though I would miss the chuckles to be had from
what the Queen would call their 'silly twittering', if
I had a bedchamber to myself.

My own new gown has already been whisked off
to be altered for a special celebration tomorrow –
which means that no one is taking any notice of
me (though, with new gowns to be cooed over or
critiqued, that is not surprising), so what better time
to start my latest daybooke? If Mrs Champernowne,

the Mistress of the Maids, comes in now, she will merely think I am most pious and doing just as she said when she gave me this beautiful blue vellum book at New Year.

'This is not for your usual scribbles, Grace,' she told me as she handed it over. (She had seen my eyes light up at the sight of it and knows how I love to write.) 'It is for quiet thoughts and meditations. You are nearly fifteen now and not supposed to act like a child.'

Well, *I* don't think I act like a child, whatever Mrs Champernowne may think. I hardly ever climb trees any more (last Tuesday does not count because it was only a very small tree) or go racing down passageways, and I am certain that I do not have my giggling fits in front of her. But all the same, I was very pleased to have a new daybooke. I have kept it empty for two whole weeks, waiting to write about a very important occasion that is about to occur. Twelve years ago tomorrow, Her Majesty Queen Elizabeth – my godmother and most favourite person in the world – was crowned Queen of England. And there is to be a grand celebration commemorating the wonderful event. She has invited a great number of foreign dignitaries to come and share in the festivities. Tomorrow there will be a procession, with the Queen dressed exactly as she was at her coronation.

I wish I had been old enough to see her crowned but I was only two at the time. Mrs Champernowne says it was the most wonderful day of her life – watching the Queen ascend the throne. She says Her Majesty looked very regal and composed. Well, she looks very composed on every occasion, except when she loses her temper. Then we all duck!

It is strange to be at Placentia during the winter, yet this is the second year we have visited in January. Last year we came because there was talk of the plague – which was most unlikely in the cold weather, but the rumours still sent the whole Court scurrying down the river to Greenwich. This year, so Mary Shelton tells me, Her Majesty has decided not to hold her coronation celebrations at Whitehall Palace, where we would usually be at this time, because last winter the River Thames froze solid. I remember this very well, as there was a Frost Fair on the frozen river, and all the Maids were able to race about on skates (with varying success!). The Queen hopes that as Placentia is further east and nearer the sea, the river is less likely to freeze, which means that all the foreign

ambassadors and their retinues will be able to arrive on the water in their barges, thus getting the most impressive view of the very palace where she was born.

Although we have known about tomorrow's celebrations for a long time – they seem to be the only thing that anyone is talking about at Court – we had no idea that they would cause us to be roused from our beds even earlier than usual this morning. The first I knew of it was hearing Mrs Champernowne's sweet Welsh tones.

'Make haste, make haste!' she said, giving us all a shake. 'The Queen wishes you to attend her without delay.'

We stumbled from our beds, bleary-eyed (I doubt there is a single Maid at Court who could truthfully say she ever got enough sleep – even when I haven't been out on Her Majesty's secret business, I wake up as stiff as a statue from tiredness). The bedchamber was very dark – it was not yet six o'clock – and there were patterns of frost all over the windows. The fires had not long been lit so the glass was chilled. Mrs Champernowne trotted off to wake the other Maids and our tiring women came to get us dressed. I was just rubbing my eyes and listening to

Sarah complain about the early hour when Ellie Bunting, my tiring woman, appeared before me with my clothes.

'She don't know what early is, Grace,' Ellie whispered as she laced on my sleeves. 'When I was a laundry maid, I was up long before this each day – and only abed at midnight. And I never saw a fire close to!'

I remembered how thin and tired Ellie used to be from her work in the laundry, and how I could do nothing about it, for I was not allowed to mix with so-called 'commoners'. All I could do was smuggle food to her whenever I was able. I will never forget how happy I was that day last year, when Her Majesty honoured Ellie for her part in solving a mystery that had troubled the Court. She was made my tiring woman – which meant that we could finally speak in public! Our friend Masou was also honoured for his part – he was made a Queen's fool (and quickly became her very favourite). But alas, I still cannot be seen associating with one of the Queen's fools, no matter how much delight he brings our Gracious Majesty, and my friendship with Masou must remain a secret. Fie, these rules are *most* silly! If only we could all mix together, lowly and highborn, life would be much more interesting.

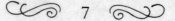

But back to the excitement of this morning. As we struggled into our clothes, there was lots of chatter about why we were being summoned so early. We do not usually see the Queen until after we have breakfasted, and so the rumours were flying around the room like a flock of noisy starlings.

'Perhaps the Queen has decided not to have her celebrations here after all,' said Mary as Olwen helped her into her petticoat.

'It would not be the first time Her Majesty has changed her mind!' agreed Sarah. Mary and I nodded. The Queen is famous for upsetting arrangements at the last minute. 'Do you think she wants us to pack up and go to Nonsuch? Or Windsor?'

'What about all the guests who are arriving at any minute?' I laughed. 'I can just imagine the whole Court being chased up and down the Thames by a host of foreign ambassadors while the Queen tries to find a palace that suits her!'

'Mayhap she is indisposed,' suggested Mary.

'Her Majesty is never ill!' declared Sarah. Then a dreamy look came over her face. 'But if she were, I suppose I would have to take her place in the procession. With my looks, and hair very much like Her Majesty's, I would be the obvious choice.'

Mary and I rolled our eyes at each other. Behind me, Ellie's brush snagged on my hair, such was her struggle to contain her chortles.

'I am sure it is nothing like illness,' I said firmly.

At that moment the other Maids burst into the room, followed by servants with some bread and small beer so that we could break our fast.

'Sarah!' Lady Jane Coningsby gasped in mock horror. 'Are you not ready yet? Make haste, or Her Majesty will be angry.'

She is a fine one to talk. She and Sarah take more time over their appearance than any of the other Maids.

Sarah had just opened her mouth to make a retort when Carmina Willoughby butted in.

'You will hurry when you hear why we have been summoned,' she said, her eyes sparkling with excitement. She broke off a piece of bread and waved it at us. 'Lucy has heard such news! Tell them, Lucy.'

Lucy Throckmorton has not long been a Maid of Honour at Court but she seems to know everything. At least she *thinks* she does, which makes Carmina hang on her every word.

Lucy drew herself up, tilting her chin in the air

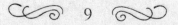

9

slightly, doing her best to look very important. 'The Queen is to marry,' she announced. 'She has accepted the proposal of the French King's son, Henri, Duc d'Anjou.'

Carmina nodded vigorously at her side. 'And we are to be the first to know!'

I could not believe what I was hearing. Surely this could not be true. I knew Secretary Cecil had been negotiating for this but had not realized it had gone quite so far. Besides, the Duc d'Anjou has insulted Her Majesty. He has been heard to say that she is old.

'It will be a summer wedding,' Lucy continued, chin still tilted.

'The Queen must want to tell us of it herself,' breathed Carmina, wide eyed with excitement.

Sarah gave herself a last glance in her looking glass and shooed away her tiring woman, Fran. 'Then we have no time for breakfast,' she announced grandly. 'Her Majesty needs us immediately!'

Sarah must have been most keen to find out more, for there is very little that comes between her and her beautifying.

I grabbed a hunk of bread as Sarah bustled us to the door. I was certainly not going to go without food, no matter what news awaited us.

As I nibbled on the bread, I found myself feeling quite anxious. The Queen is doing a marvellous job ruling England on her own – I could not imagine her wanting to share her power with a king. If the Queen *must* marry, then it will be for the good of England and, alas for her, not for love. If she could choose the man she most cared for, it would certainly not be the Duc d'Anjou but Robert Dudley, my Lord of Leicester. However, I think that will never be . . .

Mrs Champernowne was chivvying us along a hallway when Jane stopped at the window.

'Look at the young men fishing!' she called.

The other Maids crowded round the window. I had no intention of gawping at any courtiers but found myself carried along in the tide. There was a group of gentlemen standing on the bank of the river. We could see in the flickering torchlight that they had rods and lines.

'Who would go fishing at this hour,' exclaimed Sarah with a shiver, 'except for a wager?'

'Maybe we have time to go and ask if they have caught anything,' said Jane wistfully. Jane never misses an opportunity to speak to the young men of the Court.

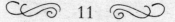

'Girls,' fussed Mrs Champernowne. 'Come away from there! The Queen will not wait while you swoon over every young man you see!'

She marched us down to the Presence Chamber almost at a run. The Queen must have heard us panting and shuffling outside the door, for her commanding tone to enter rang out before the guards had had the chance to announce us. We all fell silent. It was impossible to predict her mood from her tone.

The doors were swung open and we walked in as sedately as we could and curtsied deeply. The Queen was surrounded by her Ladies-in-Waiting. She was seated on her grand chair of bright gold and carved vine leaves and salamanders. When I was young, I would sit here while my mother and Her Majesty had long conversations; I would soon lose interest in their words and pretend that the little lizards were my pets and I was feeding the leaves to them. Her Majesty motioned for us to sit on our cushions at her feet. I noticed that all the Maids looked relieved – the Queen seemed to be in good humour.

'I am sure you are all wondering why you are called from your beds so early,' she said with a smile. 'I have summoned you all here for a very special reason.'

I had a moment of panic. Her Majesty's eyes were dancing with delight. Surely she would not look like this if she was going to marry? Unless she was actually in love, like Lady Sarah and Mr Daniel Cheshire. What a terrible thought – the Queen moping around, writing dreadful poems about the moon. (She usually writes beautiful poetry, but love seems to make everyone silly.)

'We are awaiting a very special delivery,' the Queen went on. I think everyone must have heard my sigh of relief. Husbands do not get delivered! 'I wish everybody to look their most splendid for my coronation celebration tomorrow – so I have commanded the Keeper of the Great Wardrobe to bring a number of my gowns here to Placentia. These are gowns that I myself have worn in the past to some momentous events and occasions. Each of my Maids and Ladies-in-Waiting is to choose the one that best suits her.'

Everyone's face lit up at this news – at least, everyone's but mine. I could not believe my ears. We had been summoned to the Queen just to choose new clothes! And before breakfast, to boot! I am not interested in what I wear, and anyway, I have plenty of clothes that would have done for tomorrow's festivities. I would have been quite happy to stay warm and snug in bed, sending Ellie in my place. Ellie has an eye for fashion – all the Maids clamour for her help with colour and style.

'I am justly proud of my Court,' the Queen was saying, 'and as you know, many foreign guests will have their eyes on us. We must make a splendid show, for I would remind our neighbours of England's strength and splendour.'

Of course, I didn't want to let my beloved godmother down, especially in front of all our neighbours – but I was certain I could look perfectly fine in my blue silk gown with the flowery sleeves.

The doors swung open and Sir John Fortescue, the Keeper of the Great Wardrobe, swept in, followed by some stern-looking guards in Tower livery. This was peculiar, I thought – what use could a bunch of giggling, twittering Maids and Ladies have for such strong security?

Sir John bowed low before the Queen. Behind him came servant after servant, staggering under the weight of enormous trunks. They were placed around the floor under the watchful eye of Sir John, who indicated precisely where each one should go. He then took off the heavy padlocks and withdrew. As he left, our tiring women entered.

I saw the excitement on Ellie's face. She curtsied to the Queen, but could barely keep her eyes off the trunks. I was hoping she would sort my needs out quickly and get it over with. The thought of spending all morning discussing fashion made my eyelids droop.

The Maids and Ladies could barely contain themselves. Carmina wriggled on her cushion like an excited worm. Sarah and Jane started disagreeing about the colours they should choose, and Lucy and Mary jumped to their feet in their eagerness to dive into the trunks. I sighed. It was going to be a tedious morning.

'Enough!' shouted the Queen. 'You are Maids of Honour to the Queen of England, not a gaggle of silly geese! Now make your choices' – she glared at Jane and Sarah – 'and we will brook no squabbling.'

There was immediate silence and we all rose. I noticed that everyone was struggling to be as calm as possible. Every Maid knew that if Her Majesty was upset now, there would be no gowns for choosing, however important they might be to England's splendour!

The trunks were flung open and the Maids all crowded round to gasp and sigh as each gown was brought out. Ellie disappeared in the crush, and I

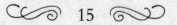

realized I would have to wait for her attentions.

'Did you ever see such delicate lace!' Lady Jane was exclaiming as Fran held up a beautiful pair of sleeves for her inspection.

'I think I shall burst!' squealed Carmina, earning a frown from the Queen. 'Come, Lucy,' she added in a slightly lower tone, 'let's have a look in each trunk before we decide. We do not want to miss anything.'

'But Olwen has just found a beautiful painted silk,' protested Lucy. 'I shall start with that, before Jane sees it. It is just the sort of thing she would think suits her, although I am sure *I* would look better in it.'

She marched off. Carmina flitted from one trunk to the next like a butterfly on a buddleia bush. There was a bewildering choice of exquisite garments in rich velvet, deep-coloured silk and fine satin. There were also several trunks of ruffs, partlets, stomachers and hats. The Queen is often given gifts of clothing and I am certain that much of it is never worn. I tried to picture all the careful packing and the procession of carts that must have brought the Queen's clothes from the house near Baynard's Castle where the Great Wardrobe stores them. I wondered what Mr Fyshe and his tailors would say

when they found they had a mountain of gowns to alter for tomorrow. I suspected they would be up all night.

I saw Ellie staggering past, her arms piled high with ruffs. She was making for Sarah. I would have to wait even longer for her attention while my fussy lady scrutinized them. In truth I am very pleased that my dear friend has taken to her tiring woman's job so well – and thank Heaven for it, as I have not the mental will to endure endless discussions about how I should wear my hair or sleeves to match the latest French or Spanish fashion. I am quite happy to let Ellie take care of all that business.

Three smaller chests stood unnoticed in the corner of the chamber. I could see that they had not been opened and I groaned inwardly. Did we really need any more gowns to be fussed over? Yet, upon closer inspection, these had a different appearance from the open trunks – less elaborate and stronger looking. I idly ran my finger over the carved crest on the top of one, wondering what further delights the Maids would find inside to squeal at, when a sudden sharp voice close behind made me jump.

'Move aside, my lady.'

I turned to see a heavily armed guard wearing

the Tower livery looking fiercely down at me. I moved back in surprise as five more guards, each armed with swords and pikes (they looked most menacing), lifted the chests and marched out of the chamber with them.

Intrigued, I glanced over at Her Majesty, wondering why she had ordered these particular chests to be taken away. Had she too tired of all the fussing? The Queen saw my puzzled look and beckoned me to her. She can read me so well! I curtsied low and she took my hands and drew me up with an amused smile.

'I must congratulate you, Grace,' she said so that no one else could hear. 'I see you have spotted the very thing I wished to keep secret. The chests taken away just now have gone to a closely guarded room. They contain my coronation crown and jewels. I intend to wear them tomorrow. You must not tell anyone of this yet, Grace. I did not want it put about that this precious cargo was being transported from the Tower. There are those who would relieve me of it on the way!'

I had a sudden picture in my head of a dark, stormy scene and a huge band of barbaric brigands leaping out on the unsuspecting Tower guards. I imagined the grisly villains sneaking off with the

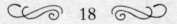

chests, leaving the gallant guards bleeding to death on the road. Then I realized I was woolgathering and must listen to the Queen.

'I ordered the gowns to be fetched from my Wardrobe,' she was saying, 'and the carts to make a second stop at the Tower. The jewels were to be added to the load. Only the most trusted Tower guards were privy to the ploy.'

'So the trunks of clothes masked their arrival,' I whispered. 'How clever, Your Majesty!'

The Queen smiled. 'Not clever enough to slip by your sharp eyes, my dear god-daughter.'

I felt my cheeks flush with pride.

The Queen was looking wryly at the Maids and Ladies milling around the array of garments which now spilled out of the trunks, or were laid out on sheets on the floor.

'I should be pleased that the ruse has worked on everyone else,' she said. Then she sighed. 'But I sometimes despair that the Ladies of the English Court seem so dull-witted.'

I was not sure how to answer this – for some certainly are! Then a happy thought came to me.

'All must seem so compared with their Queen,' I said with a curtsy.

This was not idle flattery. Her Majesty is the

cleverest person I have ever known.

'Go, Grace,' said the Queen, patting my hand in delight at the compliment. 'I can see a certain friend – or rather, tiring woman – of yours waving a gown at you.'

Ellie was standing at a respectful distance with a garment over one arm. In the other she held a partlet and some matching sleeves. Good, I thought. Now I would not have to sift through all these fine clothes. She had done the work for me – and it seemed she was enjoying herself, for she had a broad smile.

'That is a good choice, Ellie,' I said as I joined her. 'It will look well.'

Her smile vanished. Now I was confused – how could that have been the *wrong* thing to say?

'How can you be sure, Grace?' she asked. 'You've got to see the others first. There are two gowns of rich brown crushed velvet with diamond embroidery, one of white silk with gold thread, and another you might remember, for Her Majesty wore it last New Year – not this one just gone but twelve months since.'

Ellie scarcely drew breath as she led me between the twittering Maids and Ladies to one of the

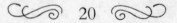

trunks. 'It's a most beautiful gown of shimmering black satin.'

'Mmmmm!' I murmured, trying to sound interested.

'It's cut all over and lined with white sarsenet,' she gabbled in her excitement, 'and it's embroidered with beautiful clouds and skylarks and the sleeves are cut and lined underneath with white taffeta.'

'Oooh,' I said, feeling that some answer was required.

'And there are little pearls sewn all over the skirts and the hem. Oh, it's such a lovely thing, you can't imagine. You'll know it when you see it. You said you specially liked it at the time.'

I just wanted Ellie to tell me quickly which gown was the finest so the thing would be over. But I realized that I must pretend to consider my choice most seriously if I did not wish to irk her. I frowned, felt all the fabrics of the gowns, frowned again and held each colour up to my cheek for her inspection.

'The velvet brings out the colour of your eyes,' mused Ellie, standing back to consider.

I nodded wisely. 'I believe you are right.'

'But the green silk with the stomacher covered in silken roses is so delicate . . .'

'So delicate,' I repeated with great solemnity.

Ellie pursed her lips and put her head on one side as she watched me running my fingers vaguely over one of the brown gowns.

'Well, if you're not going to choose, I'll have to do it for you,' snorted Ellie, thrusting the black satin gown at me. 'This is the one that will suit you best.' She sighed. 'I don't know what you'd do without me.'

Mary Shelton caught her eye and she bustled off importantly.

I realized that a whispered commotion had broken out behind me. I turned to see Jane and Sarah standing on opposite sides of one of the trunks, hands on hips and chins stuck out in fury. Between them lay a gown of deep crimson velvet. Everyone had gathered round to listen as they hissed at each other, as loudly as they could without Her Majesty overhearing.

'I saw it first!' Jane was saying. 'So I shall have it.'

'The only reason to let you take it would be out of pity,' returned Sarah, red in the face. 'After all, you have no admirer, while I have Daniel, who would praise whatever I was wearing.'

'He would more likely *laugh* if he saw you in that colour,' Jane whispered crossly.

'This was one of Her Majesty's gowns,' Sarah whispered back haughtily. 'If it suited her it will look very fine on me, for our hair is very similar.' She tossed her curls.

'The Queen does not look like a carrot!' snapped Jane.

I stifled a giggle. There has lately been hardly any bickering between my two jealous ladies. Daniel Cheshire is hopelessly in love with Sarah and these days she scarcely bothers to reply to Jane's barbed comments. I know it is wicked of me, but I must admit, I have missed the fun.

Mrs Champernowne pushed past me through the crowd. Before Sarah could make a retort she took both Maids firmly by the arm. 'Lady Jane! Lady Sarah!' she said. 'Remember who you are and stop behaving like a couple of fishwives! There are gowns aplenty and no need to argue.'

Sarah and Jane looked daggers at each other over Mrs Champernowne's panting bosom.

'The Queen has ordered me to take you to have these wonderful dresses fitted and sent for alterations,' the Mistress of the Maids went on. 'If we delay any longer they will not be ready by tomorrow.'

We made our thanks to the Queen, who luckily

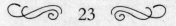

had not heard the rumpus, and curtsied our way out of the Presence Chamber. Mary Shelton and I were the first to our bedchamber. There was even less room than usual with our tiring women and two of Mr Fyshe's tailors inside. The tailors had only just started pinning up Mary's hem when we heard a loud ripping sound from the passageway outside, followed by a shriek. I ran to the door with Ellie. Mary followed, scattering pins as she went.

I warrant we all thought we were dreaming when we saw the cause of the noise. Jane stood clutching the crimson velvet gown that she and Sarah had been arguing about. Sarah had a large, torn piece of its bodice dangling from her hand. My two ladies must have had a veritable battle, for it is no easy feat to rip such strong seams apart. I heard Ellie suppress a cry of anguish. She treats all the gowns as if they are her children. She must have felt as if one was being tortured before her very eyes.

'See what you've done, you clay-brained gudgeon!' hissed Sarah.

'I?' retorted Jane. 'You were the one who chose to play tug-of-war.'

Sarah flung the ripped piece of fabric at her. 'I do believe this will suit you better than me, Jane,'

she said furiously. She pushed past us into our bedchamber and threw herself onto her bed, where she sat and glowered at us all. 'I didn't want it anyway,' we heard her mutter.

Ellie scampered off as I was being pulled about by one of Mr Fyshe's tailors. I wondered where she had gone, but by the time my fitting was done and my gown taken away, she was back with some garments in her hands.

She placed them lovingly on the bed next to the sulking Sarah. 'I think you will find this most flattering, my lady,' she said, presenting her with a fine gown of deep blue and gold.

Sarah's pout was gone in an instant. 'Thank you, Ellie,' she gasped, holding the gown up in front of her as she gazed into the looking glass. A naughty smile spread over her face. 'It is perfect. I cannot wait to see Jane's envious looks when she sees me in this!'

'And here is something for you, Lady Grace,' said Ellie, more politely than usual, because other people were listening. She put a black velvet cloak round my shoulders. It felt lovely and warm. 'It's lined with coney fur. It'll go a treat with your gown.' She leaned down to me. 'And if you get any young courtiers saying sweet things to you,' she whispered,

digging me in the ribs, 'send 'em to me. I'm the one who chose all your clothes, so I'm the one who should hear the fine words!'

'I promise,' I whispered back, 'that I will send every one your way.'

When Ellie had finished with me I tucked myself into the corner where I am now, and started writing in my daybooke. I could hear the fitters having a deal of trouble persuading Sarah the gown she had claimed was perfect not a minute ago truly was the right length, and the sleeves would be just so, and she would look very fine indeed. I caught one of them making a face behind her back and wanted to laugh. It was only when Mary said that all heads — especially Daniel's — would turn as soon as she entered the Great Hall that Sarah was satisfied.

Her gown was taken away with Mary's (a lovely cream-coloured one with little rubies sewn into it) for the alterations to be made and linings to be replaced. No sooner had they gone than Sarah began to have her doubts again. Was the ruff right for the gown? Were the sleeves a touch too wide for the fashion? She was sure Jane would have something to say if they were.

I will keep my head in my daybooke! I do not

want to be asked my opinion. It is sure to be wrong and will enrage Sarah further. And we do not want any more torn gowns . . .

Ellie might faint in distress!

A little later

Sarah was still dressing after the fitting, with both Olwen and Fran to help, when Mrs Champernowne put her head round the door.

'Hurry now, girls,' she said. (Life is one big hurry to Mrs Champernowne!) 'We are to go to the Privy Chamber to help Her Majesty dress before she receives her guests.' Then she disappeared again.

Mary smiled as she adjusted her hat. 'These guests will give Lucy and Carmina much to gossip about,' she said. 'I am sure we will hear more about their plans for the Queen's supposed marriage to Henri, Duc d'Anjou.'

'They can gossip and plan all they like,' I said hotly. 'I am certain the Queen will never agree to such an alliance.'

'She *is* nearly twice his age,' put in Sarah.

'It is true that she is thirty-seven and he is only nineteen,' I retorted, 'but that does not excuse him from insulting the Queen of England.'

If I was her I would shut the ports and keep him out.

Amomentlater

Mrs Champernowne's red face has just appeared again — and she's told me off for holding everyone up! She has scuttled off to chivvy the others now. I must stop writing. I am sure our poor harassed mother hen will tut at me all the way to the Privy Chamber. I shall tell her that I was writing about the dresses — which is true — with a prayer 'giving grateful thanks for Her Majesty's goodness and generosity to me, an unworthy Maid'. That is also true as I have just written it!

Eleven of the clock, in the Glass Gallery

I have snatched up my daybooke and come here to

the Glass Gallery – where I can be alone, I hope. No matter that my alcove is far from a fire. I must suffer and shiver if I wish to remain hidden. Something has happened which has shaken the very foundations of the Court and I must make an entry while I can. It is not likely to be my last today.

Mrs Champernowne chivvied us along to the Queen's Privy Chamber and we helped the Queen dress in one of her most beautiful gowns: a rich vermilion with quilted sleeves, slashed to show rose silk underneath. After a long look in the glass, she gave a pleased nod and led the way out of her Privy Chamber and into the Presence Chamber. Although I was several paces behind, I could see that all eyes in the room were on the wondrous spectacle that she made. And there were a lot of eyes. Faith, the place was awash with ambassadors! (I knew that it would be, but the sight of them all together did make me start!) Some of them looked very tired from all the travel.

I was burning to find out if any of the guests were the Queen's intended husband but I would have been chided for gossiping. Instead I craned forward when anyone approached the Queen, in case any betrothal rings or gifts were exchanged, but I saw nothing.

Sir William Cecil, Her Majesty's Secretary, came up to the Queen and bowed deeply before introducing the foreign visitors one by one. Mary Shelton was by my side. 'It will be easy to see who is from which country by the way they behave,' she whispered. 'If their fashions are not clue enough.'

'Let us play at guessing at their nationalities,' I whispered back. 'It will pass the time.'

Some of the other Maids nodded enthusiastically at my suggestion.

'Mijnheer Fonteinbloom,' announced Secretary Cecil.

'Dutch!' hissed Mary quickly. 'See how he fawns over Her Majesty.'

She was right. Mr Fonteinbloom almost kissed the hem of the Queen's skirt. The Hollanders are hoping she will become an important ally to them in their war against Spain. The rest of his retinue followed suit with comical low bows.

'Spanish!' giggled Carmina from my other side as the next name was called.

'Unfair!' I told her. 'We have seen him before – and not long ago.'

We all remembered this gentleman from his visit

to the Court at the time of St Bartholomew's Fair.
Don Guerau de Spes bowed stiffly. He seemed
determined to appear polite, but there was an
arrogance about him as usual. I looked up and
down the Presence Chamber to see if he had
brought his unspeakable aunt, La Doña Isabella de
Spes, but there was no sign of her. The rest of the
Spanish retinue came forward and then went back
to their places, but not before they had sent
murderous looks towards the Dutch contingent.
The Hollanders glared back in turn. The Spanish
ladies then made a great show of swishing their
skirts (made of fine silks and satins, I noted – since
Ellie would not be seeing the procession of
glamorous foreigners, I was doing my best to record
everything in my mind so that I could give her the
fullest account of all the fashions). The Dutch ladies,
for their part, were well dressed – if a little dull –
but the Spaniards obviously thought they looked
better. For a moment I wondered if warfare might
break out in the Great Hall!

The next visitor stepped up.

'French!' I said before either of the other two
Maids could. But I did not manage to say it as
quietly and earned myself a reproachful look from
Mrs Champernowne – though I would wager

she would have joined in our game if she could!

I was right. Secretary Cecil announced Monsieur de la Mothe-Fénelon, the French Ambassador. He was accompanied by a horde of gentlemen and ladies, all holding themselves proud and aloof from the English.

'I would like to say something disdainful about their clothes,' Mary said in my ear, 'but I can find only words of admiration, more's the pity. Look at their fine lattice partlets.'

Even I had to admit that the intricate lace at their necks was beautiful. The Queen favours the French fashion, or 'vogue' as the French call it – which was one in the eye for the Spanish!

Carmina suddenly pulled at my sleeve. 'Which one is Henri, Duc d'Anjou?'

I scanned the faces but could not see anyone like the portrait that had been sent to the Queen when the betrothal had been suggested. 'Is the Duc here?' I passed the question on to Mary.

'No,' she answered, with her hand in front of her mouth in case the Mistress of the Maids was looking our way again. 'There is no sign of him.'

I was glad of it. The man is not good enough for our wonderful Queen and I wish I could tell her so. Who does he think he is to insult our sovereign?

But it is not for me to get involved. Her Majesty must see some good reason for such a marriage or she would not even countenance the discussions. And at least for now there would be no more talk of Henri, Duc d'Anjou.

The line of dignitaries waiting to greet the Queen seemed endless. Dukes and barons and messieurs and signors from everywhere had come to Court. If Secretary Cecil had announced the man in the moon, I would have nodded as if that were completely expected. At last, the final Ambassador had made his homage and Secretary Cecil turned to all the assembled people – so numerous that it made the vast Presence Chamber seem like a cupboard! Secretary Cecil had plans to alleviate this, and his words caused quite a stir amongst us all.

'One of the crowns that graced Her Majesty's royal head on the day of her coronation, twelve glorious years ago, is on display for all to see.' There was an excited murmuring at this. But the Queen's loyal minister had not finished. He held up a hand for silence. 'Along with the orb and sceptre that she held in the sight of us all, to show her right to be our Sovereign.'

'One of the crowns?' whispered Carmina,

looking puzzled. 'What does he mean? Surely Her Majesty did not wear two crowns at once!' She turned to Lucy for an answer.

Lucy did not disappoint. 'The Queen wore three crowns in turn,' she told us. 'As her sister Mary and brother Edward did at their coronations. She wore the crown of St Edward to begin with, as all monarchs have done since the time of Edward the Confessor. But it is very heavy, and was removed after the vows. It was replaced with the imperial crown, and then finally with the one we see her wear at times. It is much lighter.' She made her eyes go all misty with emotion. As the newest Maid of Honour she seems to think she must work extra hard to show how loyal she is to the Queen. I do not mean to be unkind, but her earnestness is quite annoying. 'It is the crown of St Edward that is to be on display, for it is the sacred symbol of the moment she became Queen.'

'Ooh!' said Carmina.

'But that's not *all* the story,' added Mary Shelton. She bent her head nearer so that only us Maids could hear. 'She is wearing the crown for the Hollanders' benefit.' When we all looked at her in confusion, Mary continued: 'I had it from my aunt, whose cousin's husband works for Secretary Cecil –

Her Majesty is raising a loan to give money to the Dutch for their fight against the Spanish. The crown of St Edward is to be held in surety for this loan. She wants the Hollanders to see how valuable the crown is so that they know she is as good as her word.'

I could see where this was going. 'And the Spanish,' I put in, 'will be able to see that she is secretly – or not so secretly – supporting the Dutch, whose country they have invaded.'

'Exactly!' Mary gave a laugh of pleasure. 'They will be unable to say anything about it. They must stand there and smile through their fury.'

We had heard grim tales of Spanish cruelty against the Dutch people. It made me shiver at times, for they might turn their attention to England next. Of course, Her Majesty would not stand for that.

Secretary Cecil was just coming to the end of a long speech. He had gone into great detail about how the viewing would take place. The Queen looked very satisfied. The wearing of her crown jewels tomorrow and the display of them today was a demonstration of England's power.

'I invite you to come and see the splendour for yourselves,' he finished solemnly and walked to the

door, where he was joined by another man whom I had not seen before.

'Do you know who that is?' I whispered to Mary Shelton.

'That is Tobias Bennett,' Mary whispered back. 'He is the Jewel Master of the Tower of London. If this goes well, be sure he will become *Sir* Tobias.'

I knew that Jewel Master was an important position, and Tobias certainly had a serious look on his face. What a responsibility to have the precious jewels here in the palace and not safely back at the Tower! I wondered how he had felt, having to let the jewels travel with the Queen's gowns and not under his protection. For, if he had been seen accompanying the chests, it would have aroused suspicion that mayhap the jewels were there as well.

A crowd of Ambassadors and their ladies followed him at once. We Maids were all very eager to go, but of course, he had to attend Her Majesty.

'I hope we shall get to see them soon,' whispered Carmina.

'I am happy to wait a while,' said Jane. 'It will be even more of a crush there than here. All the Dutch have gone and so have the French.'

'You are right,' I said, with mischief intended, I admit. 'What with the scores of Gentleman Guard

to keep the jewels safe, there will be barely room to breathe.'

Jane's eyes lit up at the thought of being squeezed in with the Gentlemen Guard. 'But we must go too at the first opportunity, so as not to miss out on anything!'

By now the first visitors to the jewels were trickling back into the Presence Chamber and were surrounding the Queen, making pretty speeches about the wonderful crown. One lady was squeaking about the rubies sparkling in the candlelight.

'When will it be our turn?' hissed Jane impatiently.

'You must be patient for a while yet, Lady Jane.' It was the Queen! Poor Jane turned as red as a radish. But to everyone's relief, the Queen was smiling. 'Though I am pleased that you are eager to see my jewels.'

It was not long before the Presence Chamber seemed very full again and no one was making for the door. Did that mean everyone had now seen the jewels? It might be our turn. I decided to be bold.

'May we go now, Your Majesty?' I asked.

The Queen laughed. 'I am sorry to disappoint,'

she said. 'You will have your turn, I promise; but for now, we have some manner of small spectacle to watch.'

I heard Jane stifle a groan. I was glad that we were sitting with the Queen and therefore were afforded some space, for Mr Somers, the leader of the Queen's troupe of acrobats, had appeared in the centre of the chamber and was hustling people out of the way, albeit very politely. Some of the dignitaries looked very squashed indeed!

Mr Somers addressed the crowd. 'Make way for Her Majesty!' he announced.

Some of the foreigners shared puzzled looks. The Queen was already there – they could see her with their own eyes! What was this man talking about? Then two harbingers entered the room and sounded their horns just as if Her Majesty herself was outside the chamber, ready to enter. At once I could see these were no ordinary harbingers but Peter and Paul, the dwarf twins. And behind them, his dark-skinned face covered in white lead, came Masou, walking regally. He had a sparkling gold crown perched atop a red wig. He was trying to put on a 'royal' expression, but to me it just made him look as if he was sucking lemons. I must remember to tell Ellie about it. She will laugh – unlike my

Lady Jane, who tapped her foot impatiently as the troupe performed.

'The crown is made of glass jewels and gilt paper, I'll warrant,' Mary Shelton whispered to me, earning a harsh look from Lady Jane, who seemed completely unwilling to enjoy the performance as long as it delayed her viewing of the jewels.

The rest of the troupe scampered in behind Masou. They were dressed like foreign noblemen and represented the visitors to the Court, all in awe of their glorious Queen. They bowed and scraped behind their 'Sovereign' in a most comical manner – especially little Gypsy Pete, who kept tripping on a cloak that was far too long for him. I do not know if he meant to, but it made us all laugh – especially because the long cloak was in the Spanish style! I could see many of Don Guerau's people frowning at this, although the Ambassador himself gave nothing away. Mr Somers had not *actually* said that the spectacle was to show England as more powerful than the rest of Europe, and if the visitors thought this and were offended, then they were just being silly.

Masou beckoned to French Louis, who was dressed as a Lady-in-Waiting, despite his thick black beard. He held a tray piled high with silk-wrapped parcels. Together they went up to the Ambassadors and Masou presented each one with the rich-looking gifts. I knew these must be from the Queen herself.

Then the spectacle was over. French Louis picked up Masou's train and they departed to great applause.

At last it was our turn to see the crown, orb and sceptre. The Queen beckoned to the Jewel Master. He came at once to her summons and bowed deeply.

'Mr Bennett,' she said. 'My Maids wish to see the jewels now and I will come as well. I look forward to seeing the wonder on their faces. They are all too young to remember the actual coronation.'

The Jewel Master beamed. 'What an honour, Your Majesty!' He bowed again and then waited for the Queen to lead the way out of the Presence Chamber, but she asked him to escort her along the passageway. The man was so pleased he looked as if he'd been *given* the crown jewels.

We followed, and Secretary Cecil came behind, murmuring pleasantries to Mrs Champernowne. The jewels were being kept in one of the armoury storerooms. I remembered now that last week I had seen servants carrying armour about the palace.

They must have been emptying the chamber ready for the display.

'I do not like to contradict Her Majesty,' whispered Sarah, 'but I *do* remember the coronation, every moment.'

'Then you must be a lot older than you claim,' hissed Lady Jane waspishly. 'Of course, that would explain your weathered skin.'

Sarah gave her a glare full of daggers and I thought she might pinch Jane even in the Queen's presence. Mary Shelton quickly moved between them.

'I am sure that children were not allowed in Westminster Abbey,' she said soothingly. 'But you were probably told all about the ceremony, Sarah, and so you remember it as if you'd been there.'

Mr Bennett gave the Queen a small bow and then came back to walk with us. 'Her Majesty wishes me to give you a description of the sight you are about to see,' he told us. 'St Edward's crown is truly awe-inspiring. Its band is encrusted with twelve precious stones. It has two gold arches with a cross above, from which hang delicate pearls.'

'I would love to wear such a thing,' sighed Sarah. 'I remember thinking so at the time,' she added, with a pointed look at Jane, who just glared back.

The Jewel Master smiled at Sarah. 'But you would not want to wear it for long, my lady. The gold and jewels make it most weighty.'

We were about to turn into the passage that led to King Henry's armouries when we heard the real harbingers sound their trumpets to alert all that the Queen was coming. It was a much more forceful sound than the dwarf twins had made on their horns.

The passage was lined with about twenty of the Gentlemen Guard. They all stood to attention as the Queen passed. They were an impressive sight and it did my heart good to know that the jewels were so safely guarded. Lady Jane would have liked to have lingered and conversed (flirted!), I am sure, but, of course, she could not.

We reached the storeroom and I entered just behind the Queen. She swept straight in towards the middle of the room, where I could see a table covered in a purple satin cloth. I felt an excited tingling in my belly – at last our eyes were going to light upon the famous crown jewels!

But the Queen suddenly stopped as if frozen to the spot. Ahead of her, two men lay slumped on the floor. They wore Tower livery and both held tankards in a loose grip. I recognized one of them as the guard who had warned me away from the jewellery chests earlier that morning. There was a jug on a table by the wall and much of the drink was spilled upon the floor.

'Drunk!' hissed Mrs Champernowne in disgust. 'And on duty as well.'

'They should be dismissed,' agreed Secretary Cecil, turning to Mr Bennett. 'Or worse.'

But Mr Bennett did not seem to hear him. He gazed in horror across the room, his mouth opening and closing silently. He raised a shaking finger and pointed at the table.

On one side of it lay the jewel-covered sceptre and on the other the orb, shining in the candlelight. All around were rings and gold bracelets. And in the middle there was . . . nothing.

'The crown,' gulped the Jewel Master, finding his voice at last. 'The crown of St Edward. It has gone!'

A few moments later

I have grown so cold that I almost could not write. To warm myself, I had to put down my daybooke and swing my arms like a windmill to get the blood

back into my fingers. Luckily no one saw me or they would think me woodwild! But I must get back to my account of today's travesty. I want to capture every detail.

We stood in the storeroom gawping like urchins at the empty space where the crown had been. All except Her Majesty. She, of course, kept her composure, but I could see that her lips were pressed tightly together and her eyes flashed with anger.

She strode over to the table where the orb and sceptre remained. I craned round and could also see a beautiful jewel-encrusted chain laid out on the satin. It was easy to see where the crown should have been. The gap glared at us. My mind started to whirl. Who could have stolen it?

'What has happened here, Mr Bennett?' said the Queen in an icy voice.

The Jewel Master's face was bright red as he hurriedly fell to his knees. I could see the sweat on his cheeks.

'Oh Gracious Queen,' he said. 'I fear to tell you the worst but it is so. The crown was here when I was last in the room. My two guards are good, trusty men.' He turned to Secretary Cecil. 'Please tend to them, sir,' he said. 'See if they still live. They are not drunk, I would wager my life on it.' He turned in desperation to us all. 'They must have been poisoned. They could only be kept from their duty by . . . death.'

His dramatic words now caused a contest of gasping and sighing from my fine ladies Jane and Sarah as they tried to outdo each other in being shocked. When Sarah sighed, Jane gasped. When Sarah wobbled and clutched the table, Jane fell against the wall breathing, 'Ah me!' in a most dramatic manner. Thankfully, one look from the Queen stopped their huffing and puffing before we were all blown away!

Secretary Cecil and Mrs Champernowne bent down to the guards. (That caused a lot more huffing and puffing, of course, as they are both rather old and stout.)

'The men are alive, Your Majesty,' said Secretary Cecil gravely. 'And methinks Mr Bennett speaks the truth, for they do not appear to be drunk.'

I was very pleased to hear that the guards were still breathing. And so too was the Queen.

'I am glad of it,' she told her minister. 'But my dear Cecil, what is to be done?'

Secretary Cecil got to his feet and went to the

door. I could see clearly what I must do. I would be a poor Lady Pursuivant indeed if I did not try to solve this shocking crime. At first sight, I had assumed that the thief had taken advantage of the guards' drunkenness. But we now knew that the guards were not drunk at all but unconscious. The thief must have done something to keep them out of his way.

Mr Cecil called in the guard who had been on duty just outside the door. It was Henry Westerland. He bowed deeply and then stood to stern attention in front of Her Majesty.

Mr Bennett started to harangue him without any deference to the Queen. 'Who has been in this room since I last left?' he demanded. 'Tell me, man!'

Henry Westerland kept his gaze straight ahead and ignored the Jewel Master.

'You may answer this question,' said the Queen in a tight voice. Mr Bennett should beware, I thought. He is forgetting himself in his panic.

'No one has entered, sir, since you left the room fifteen minutes ago with the Venetian Ambassador and his people,' said Henry Westerland. 'And no one came out.'

'No one?' Mr Bennett sounded disbelieving.

'On my honour,' said the guard. 'No one until

you came back with this esteemed party, Mr
Bennett. Your two guards remained inside and
the door was closed throughout.' He bowed to the
Queen.

So the timing of the theft was during Masou's
entertainment, I realized. I cast my mind back,
trying to think if anyone had been missing during
the display. While I was deep in thought, Mr
Bennett began haranguing Henry Westerland again.

'Fetch all the guards and search the palace,' he
ranted. 'Leave nothing unturned.'

'Mr Bennett!' said the Queen tersely. 'When I
rose from my bed this morning, I thought I was the
Monarch of England. Are you telling me I was
mistaken?' The Jewel Master visibly shrank in the
face of her sarcasm. 'I will not have you give orders
that only I can give! And I will not have you
sowing alarm and confusion in front of my guests
by having the guards storming through Placentia.'

Of course not, I thought. That would be a
disaster. All her plans for showing the strength of
England would be for nought if the guests found
out what had happened right here under the
Queen's nose.

Her Majesty turned to Henry Westerland. 'Go
quietly through the passages and seek out Mr

Hatton,' she told him. 'Ask him to come here at once and breathe not a word to anyone about what has happened here.'

Mr Westerland bowed and left the chamber. He had a look of devotion on his face and I knew he would follow his beloved Queen's instructions to the letter. It warms my heart as I write to think that Her Majesty is surrounded by such loyal men; men who would die for her. (I wish it would warm the rest of me now!)

The Jewel Master looked utterly shamefaced. I think he realized that, in his panic, he had not shown due respect to his Sovereign. He swept another bow, so deep I thought his nose would touch the floor, and then stepped back. I felt a pang of pity for the poor man. He was trying to hide his fear, but the crown had been stolen on his watch, and he must have been feeling very responsible and scared about what the Queen might do to him.

I wandered around the chamber, making sure I did not outwardly appear to take too much interest in the place. Faith, it is hard to undertake investigations when no one is supposed to know what you are doing! Everyone seems to get in the way. First I strolled about near the walls, dodging round Secretary Cecil and catching the sleeve of my gown on one of his rings. Having disentangled myself with many apologies, I finally determined that there was only one door – the one through which we had entered.

Although the armouries had been built by old King Henry, this storeroom was even older and the walls were of stone, not brick. They had been covered in whitewash especially for today's display. There were some metal sconces on the walls for the torches and for hanging the armour, but apart from that they were bare. I turned my attention to the ceiling, and nearly collided with Mrs Champernowne, who was trying in vain to calm down Jane and Sarah. While I endured her tutting, I established that the old armoury storeroom had high walls with no windows and therefore no natural light. The ceiling was covered in wooden panels. They were very old and quite ornate. An image of the sun with long beams was painted across the ceiling. As I gazed up at it, I tripped over Carmina's toe and earned myself a harsh glare from the Queen!

The Jewel Master was wringing his hands. 'This store was the perfect place to keep the jewels safe, Your Majesty,' he wailed. 'It is a strongly built room, with twenty men outside and two of my guards inside – men whose loyalty I would vouch for with my own life.' He gulped and almost choked on the words, as if he had just thought that maybe his life actually *was* at stake.

Even I could not predict what form Her Majesty's wrath would take if the crown was not recovered.

This was a puzzle indeed. Mr Westerland had said that no one had come into the room between the Court visits. I do not believe for a moment that he was lying, for I know him to be an honest man and greatly trusted by Her Majesty and Mr Hatton; and besides, he had not tried to come up with a clever story, but had simply told the bare facts. Even if I were deceived by him, there were nineteen other Gentlemen Guards in the passage outside. One of them would surely report if anybody else had come while the entertainment had been going on. How had the thief got in and out?

Faith! This puts me in mind of another mystery I was faced with last September. That time a murder had taken place inside a locked room. I found the answer then, but this is even more perplexing.

Mr Hatton arrived. He had a look of mild interest on his face. I imagine he thought he had been summoned to answer some question by one of the foreign guests – until he saw the glaring evidence before him. His expression became very grim indeed when the Queen told him all that had happened. He gave her a deep bow.

'With your permission, Your Majesty,' he said gravely, 'I will set about my investigation at once. I will hand-pick a few of my men – I know of five who will keep their mouths closed. They will search the palace, and I can trust them to do it in such a way that this dreadful crime will remain secret.'

'Mr Bennett,' said the Queen, 'I know *you* will keep silent – you have your reputation to protect for one thing.' She turned and fixed us Maids with a severe look. 'I would have you all now promise that you will not breathe a word of what has happened here.'

We all sank into deep curtsies. I knew that the Maids were too much in awe of the Queen, and had too much love and respect for her, to disobey. I noticed that she did not demand any promise from Secretary Cecil or Mrs Champernowne. She did not have to – they had known and cared for her since she was a child, and would never betray her.

Mr Hatton bent and looked at the unconscious guards. 'It would seem that whatever has floored them was in their beer,' he said.

How had it got there? I wondered. I would play the silly Maid and see if I could get some answers.

'That is terrible,' I gushed. 'The poor men were drinking poison! I wonder how it got in there.'

Mr Hatton turned at my voice and I saw him start. He glared at me and I could read his thoughts. *Not Lady Grace again. What have I done to be plagued by this meddling Maid?* I admit, he does find me underfoot (rather like a naughty puppy) whenever he is trying to solve a mystery at Court. He is a good, clever man, but not so clever that he has ever suspected my role as Lady Pursuivant. At least, he has not so far. I must be on my guard, lest I let anything slip. He must never know of it.

Mr Bennett answered my question readily (having no idea how vexed the Captain of the Guard was by my presence). 'The beer came from that flagon,' he said, pointing to a jug in the corner. 'The Tower guards work long shifts and need sustenance to keep alert.' He sighed deeply. 'There have been over a hundred visitors today. Any one of them could have dropped the poison into the beer. Though they must have been very cunning or my men, who are highly trained, would have noticed.'

I thought it was unlikely that the two guards would have noticed anyone fiddling with their drink behind their backs. Surely they would have had their eyes fixed on the jewels they were guarding.

Mr Bennett covered his eyes with his hand. 'I feel it is my fault,' he moaned. 'I told my men to take some refreshment after the last visitors had gone. I knew that the entertainment was about to begin and they would have a few moments to rest.'

Mr Hatton picked up one of the tankards and sniffed. 'It's not poison,' he announced, 'but laudanum. I can smell it. The men were drugged.'

'Then their lives are not at risk at least,' said the Queen.

'A large dose can kill a man,' Mr Hatton told her respectfully. 'But I am glad it was not so in this case. The moment they awake from their drugged stupor I can question them. They are the best witnesses to the crime that we have.'

I hoped he was also glad that the dose had not been larger for the guards' sake! But that is Mr Hatton all over. He is very practical and sticks to the job in hand.

'I will have them taken to the guardhouse by the Palace Gate,' he went on. 'They can sleep it off there and no one will see them.'

Mr Hatton was not the only one who wanted to

question the guards. I must contrive to be at the guardhouse when they awake from their stupor.

He looked impatiently around the room and I could see that he wanted to shepherd us all out of his way. But I had more questions to ask. Luckily, so did Tobias Bennett, and he had neither the tact nor the wit to see that Mr Hatton wanted us gone.

'It will be one of the foreign guests, mark my word,' the Jewel Master said ruefully.

'Whoever it is,' said the Queen, 'you must hope that they are apprehended with all speed. You are my Jewel Master and that is a position of high office. And so I hold you entirely responsible for the loss.'

Mr Bennett blanched at this. Mary whispered something to Carmina and I caught the words, '. . . bring shame upon his family.'

How true, I thought. Anyone who falls from a position of great responsibility usually takes their whole family with them.

'We must find the crown,' said Secretary Cecil in a flustered voice. 'I have told all the guests that you will wear it tomorrow and the Dutch will be expecting to see it again. The loan . . . the embarrassment . . .' His words trailed off.

'If the thief has any sense he will already be

 54

halfway to Dover by now,' said the Queen grimly.
For a brief moment I saw something in her eyes
that filled my heart with anguish. She looked
defeated. I wanted to take her hands and tell her
that I would do everything in my power to recover
her crown and find the thief, but, of course, I could
not. 'Come. We can do no good here,' she said at
last, her usual poise and composure recovered as
though they had never been absent.

She swept towards the door. As we all curtsied
deeply I saw something under the table where
the crown had been. Everyone was looking at the
Queen, so when we stood, I slipped over and
picked it up. It was a crumpled piece of parchment
and I thought to throw it away again but then saw
it had some writing on it. I faced away from the
rest of the party, straightened it out and began to
read. It was all I could do not to shout out in
surprise. The scrawling hand was in poor English,
but it must have been from the thief. It was a
poem.

They fawns upon the English Queen,
Dressed in their reds and golds and green,
And speaks fine words with their foreign tongues
But they laughing now that her crown is gone.

At the bottom was scribbled a message: *Wait for my instruction. You can be having the crown back, but I must be having something in exchange.*

I found I had been holding my breath. This thief was playing a dangerous game. He dared to hold the Queen of England to ransom! And then I felt my spirits soar. This meant the thief and the crown were still at Court. Then my spirits quickly plummeted again. That meant *anyone* could be a suspect.

I had to show the Queen this note. But not now, for we were leaving the chamber. I stuffed the parchment up my sleeve. As we walked along the passage past the Gentlemen Guard, I wondered who could possibly have smuggled the crown past twenty fine men such as these.

A ghost, mayhap. But that was a foolish thought.

The note at least gave me some clues about the thief. The English grammar was poor, as if the writer spoke only a little of our language, but the hand itself looked educated. A foreign nobleman, I thought with mounting excitement that was soon hounded away by another, more troubling thought – just how many foreign noblemen were at Court?

But I could not let that stop me. Her Majesty's

Lady Pursuivant never gives up, no matter how perplexing the mystery.

We were back in the state rooms of the palace now and I was bursting with questions. Had any of the guests acted suspiciously? No, that was foolish – the guards would have been alerted if they'd seen that. But someone might have done something unusual. I longed to ask, but I could not without alerting the Court that the crown was missing. We had promised not to let anyone else know about the theft and, indeed, Mrs Champernowne was now hurrying us along, for we had to get ready for the noontide meal, which was to be a banquet.

The Queen was setting a fast pace. I could tell from the stiff way she walked that she was working herself into a fury at the thief. Poor Lady Jane suddenly sneezed and Her Majesty jerked round at the noise. Jane looked as if she thought she might have something thrown at her, but the Queen merely turned to me.

'Lady Grace,' she said, 'you alone will come with me to my bedchamber. I wish for peace and quiet. You will comb my hair while I get ready.'

I bubbled with excitement, for I was certain I knew why she wanted me and no one else to accompany her. It must be to talk of the theft and

request my help. (She could not possibly prefer my clumsy hands to those of another maid – I have had many mishaps with the royal comb!)

We went to the Privy Bedchamber, where the Queen told all the servants to depart.

Biting my lip in concentration, I made to remove her wig. The Queen has beautiful hair, but today there would not be time for it to be styled differently to match each dress she wore, so she would wear wigs. Her Majesty stayed my hand.

'You must know why I really wanted you to accompany me,' she began, squeezing my hands in hers. 'I have seen your eyes roving about, so I know my Lady Pursuivant is already thinking of a way to solve this mystery.'

I tried to hide my astonishment that she had guessed my plans. I had thought I had given nothing away. I should have known that the Queen rarely misses anything that happens at Court.

'I know I can trust you to investigate discreetly,' she went on. 'Mr Hatton is an excellent Captain of the Guard, but he can be a little frightening and I believe sometimes people tell him what they think he wants to hear and not what he *needs* to hear.' She held up her glass and examined the kohl around her eyes. 'A Maid of Honour on the other hand can

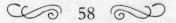

learn all sorts of things, especially one with your talents.' She put down the glass and sighed deeply. 'Though I cannot see how the crown can be recovered from this villain. Surely he is long gone by now.'

'Your Majesty,' I said quickly, 'I believe the crown is still here at Court – along with the thief, of course.'

'What say you?' she demanded.

'I found this note just as we were leaving,' I told her, and tried to pull the parchment out of my sleeve. The cursed thing stuck and I could see the Queen's shoe tapping impatiently. At last I had it free and gave it to her.

Her Majesty read the poem, a frown appearing on her face. She must have been boiling with fury, for the knuckles on her hands went white – but that was all. I marvelled at her restraint. She is truly a wonder. The smallest infringement can have her hurling a tankard across the room, but now she was keeping it all in, like a dragon preparing to blast fire. (Oh dear, I should not be comparing her to a dragon!)

'Thank you, Grace,' she said at last. 'I will show this to Mr Hatton.'

She turned and took both my hands. 'Now I

trust you not to do anything foolish or dangerous while undertaking this task for me.' She stared deep into my eyes. 'I give you permission to follow your instincts, for they are sound and true, but the moment you discover anything you must come to me.'

'I will continue in the utmost secrecy,' I vowed. 'You know I will give it my best endeavour, Your Majesty.' And then I shut my mouth. The Queen wanted me to promise not to do anything dangerous and I could not lie to her, so it was best that I said nothing at all. I never seek out danger in my role as Lady Pursuivant, but somehow it always seems to find *me*!

'Thank you, Grace.' The Queen rose and kissed my cheek. 'Ah me,' she sighed. 'I would do anything to have my crown back. How can I face the shame of not wearing it tomorrow when I have told the whole world that I will?'

'I would do anything to have this pain taken from you, Your Majesty,' I assured her. It was the first time the Queen had asked me outright to investigate on her behalf, and I was determined to see it through. 'I will not rest until this mystery is solved.'

★ ★ ★

God's oath! My hand has cramped around my quill so hard that I fear it will never move again. I must stop writing before I develop a claw.

Two of the clock

I am in my bedchamber, snatching time to write what I have discovered. There is no time to lose. I must find the Queen's crown before the celebrations tomorrow – and, if possible, bring the thief to justice. A tall order. I do not think I have ever had so few hours to solve a mystery!

Her Majesty had commanded that no one must hear of the theft, so the noontide meal was rather strained. I marvelled at the Queen, whose face did not show a trace of the anger she must be feeling. She spoke to those at table with her as if she had not a care in the world!

I felt quite sorry for Carmina and Lucy. For once, they were having trouble finding a topic of conversation. They love to make a drama out of any crisis, so perhaps they were too scared that the wrong words might escape them.

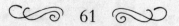

'Is it not cold today?' began Carmina in strained tones.

'I have hardly noticed,' replied Lucy, most politely.

'Neither have I, for my new cloak is wonderfully warm,' Carmina ploughed on.

'I expect it is,' said Lucy, nodding vigorously as if this was the most interesting piece of gossip in the world.

'Lady Ann has a cloak just the same,' said Carmina.

'And is it wonderfully warm too?' asked Lucy.

'I do not know,' replied Carmina. 'I have not asked her.'

'Oh,' said Lucy.

With this they both attacked their halibut and were silent.

They were trying to sound carefree – but, in truth, we were all shaken at the thought that a thief could get among us so easily.

Lady Sarah was quiet as well. She sat with Daniel Cheshire, her arm through his, eyes only for him. Daniel looked rather uncomfortable. Even though my thoughts were centred on the crime, a little niggle of worry did go through my head at this. I prayed that he was not losing interest in Lady Sarah.

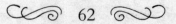

That would be a terrible thing – they are so well suited. (Putting aside all the romantic nonsense and silly poems.) Perhaps Daniel was just uncomfortable with all the strangers in the room.

I own that *I* was uncomfortable with the crowds too – but for another reason. The note had made me certain that the thief was still at Court. He could be among us at that moment – knowing full well that the Queen was waiting for his next move. What other man could claim to have such power over England's Monarch? I felt a surge of anger at the thought of the rogue revelling in his success. What if he had been an assassin? If he could sneak around and leave a note without being seen by anybody, could he have slain Her Majesty with the same ease?

I wanted to go back to the armoury store and try to find out how he had got in and see if he had left any clues as to his identity. If I had been Mr Hatton, I could have gone straight there unchallenged. But no one would let a mere Maid in. If only I could have disguised myself as the Captain of the Guard. After all, I have hidden my identity many a time as Her Majesty's Lady Pursuivant. But no, I would not pass muster, even with doublet and hose and a false beard – and I would have to walk on stilts. It was most frustrating.

I decided to concentrate instead on the thief himself for the time being. For the sweet course, we made our way to the Banqueting House where I scrutinized the guests. Was anyone behaving strangely? At first sight it seemed not. Many of the foreign dignitaries were vying for Her Majesty's attention and the rest set about insulting all things English. They would usually speak in their own language, but this time they made sure they spoke in our tongue so that we should all hear!

'It is so cold here. I am quite frozen.' This was from a sour-faced Hollander.

What cheek! I am quite certain their weather can be just as cold as ours. I have seen paintings full of snow!

'What gloomy fashions the English ladies do wear,' I heard one French lady say, flashing a nasty look at Lady Jane. That was probably jealousy – a whole flock of young men from the French Court were round Jane at the time. And it was silly of her, as most of us follow the French fashion anyway!

The sour-faced Hollander had not finished, either. 'My poor skin is sure to suffer in this wretched palace,' she remarked to her companion.

'The sheets are certain to be rough. It will be like sleeping on sand.' Ellie would have been furious to hear that. When she was a laundrymaid she was always telling me how hard she worked to keep the linen soft.

I was very glad that news of the theft had not been made public. The guests would have had some difficulty in hiding their glee! They would all be hoping it was one of their countrymen who had done the deed, no doubt. There was not a nation there which would have been anything less than delighted to get its hands on the crown of England.

With the Court packed more tightly than usual, it seemed an impossible task to investigate everyone. I ate my dessert – a rather delicious orange tart made from fruit brought as a gift by the pompous Spanish Ambassador (the man does have *some* use, I must admit), which took the theft quite out of my mind for a moment or two.

But then I found myself next to one of the Gentlemen Guard, Hugh Morling. I remembered that he had been standing on guard close to the armoury at the time of the theft. He might know if anyone had taken a special interest in the room, or behaved in an odd manner. But I could not question him directly. If he knew nothing of the theft already, I must not alert him to it. And if he *had* been told, would he know that I knew of it too? I must not be seen to be breaking my promise of silence on the matter. Oh, how to proceed?

'You have had a very special guard duty today,' I said with a smile.

Mr Morling started at my words and nearly dropped his marchpane. 'Indeed, my lady,' he said awkwardly. His eyes rapidly searched the crowd. 'You will excuse me; Mr Hatton is beckoning.'

And he went off as fast as politeness allowed. Strange, for Mr Hatton was standing with his back to us on the other side of the Banqueting House.

I concluded that Mr Morling was privy to what had happened to the crown and had no intention of letting anything slip. I searched about for a more useful source of information. My eyes fell on Samuel Twyer, who was making for a group of giggling young Frenchwomen. Well, his flirting would have to wait!

I stepped smartly out in front of him. 'Mr Twyer,' I said with another beaming smile. 'I think you must feel most honoured today.'

He looked rather taken aback at my ambush. 'Honoured, Lady Grace?' he replied. 'In what way?'

I gave a little laugh. 'How can you be so modest,

Mr Twyer?' I said playfully. 'Were you not chosen by your captain to guard the Queen's precious crown jewels?'

I watched his face for any signs of nervousness. But all I could see were some wistful glances in the direction of the French beauties. I doubted he was in Mr Hatton's confidence. Mr Twyer is something of a gossip, so perhaps the Captain of the Guard did not trust him to keep his counsel.

'I relished the duty, my lady,' he said, torn between telling me all about his honoured position and smiling at all the mademoiselles. 'Guarding the Queen's most treasured possessions – well, that was like guarding Her Majesty herself.' He said this loudly enough for the young Frenchwomen to hear – and no doubt think him brave. I could see he was anxious to get away. But he would have to put up with a few more questions first.

'Do you not think this has been the most exciting of days?' I gushed. I was playing the fluttery Maid for all I was worth. Faith, I have had so much practice at this particular role that I now act the part to perfection! 'I confess I felt a little faint with excitement at the sight of the magnificent display in the armoury store.'

'Begging your pardon,' Mr Twyer replied,

keeping his eyes on his female targets, 'but it is beyond my understanding why young ladies flock like sheep around fine jewels and coronation crowns. Indeed, one of the guests could not keep away from the display. I almost laughed to see her scurry past me for a third time. I wager the Jewel Master had to drive her out with a stick, for she was the very last to leave.'

I caught my breath at this and had to hide it with a cough. 'Pray, who was that?'

Samuel Twyer indicated a lady who had her back to us. 'I do not know her name.' The lady in question turned slightly. It was the sour-faced Hollander who had complained about the sheets. I suddenly looked at her with new eyes. Could she have been involved with the theft?

'I must go and tell the other Maids about her!' I giggled. Mr Twyer seemed most relieved that I was finally going to let him go. But his relief turned to disappointment. The French ladies had disappeared. Well, I could not worry about that. There were plenty of other young beauties for him to flirt with.

I made my way though the crowd to see what my companions knew of the Hollander. The other Maids were in a corner, deep in whispered

conversation. They jumped as I suddenly appeared among them. God's teeth! It seemed I was unnerving everyone I went near! I prayed their talk was not about the crown, for someone might overhear. But I soon found it to be a much more interesting topic – to *them*, anyway. They had been commenting on how overdressed one of the Spanish ladies was in her silver gown and how she looked down her nose at the English! I realized I might be able to turn the talk to my advantage.

'Speaking of our strange guests,' I said conspiratorially, 'have you ever seen anyone with as sour a look as the lady from the Netherlands over there?' I gave a slight nod towards the lady in question.

'Do you mean the one with the ridiculous wide skirts to her gown?' asked Carmina in delight. 'She looks as if she might fly away in a high wind. She must have the biggest farthingale in all Europe under there. Though it is probably to hide her stoutness.'

There were some muffled giggles at this.

'I wonder who she can be,' I exclaimed.

'I believe she is . . .' began Mary.

'. . . the sister-in-law to the Netherlands' Ambassador,' Lucy cut in.

'And her husband, the brother . . .' Mary tried again.

'. . . is a very rich shipping merchant,' finished Lucy in triumph.

It is a good thing Mary is so patient. At times, Lucy makes me understand why Her Majesty loves to throw shoes so often!

'I have heard that she is dreadfully spoiled,' Mary told us. 'She is indulged by her husband, who is much older than her.'

'I knew that,' said Lucy quickly.

'I wonder how she caught herself such a rich husband,' mused Jane. 'For she is no beauty. On the other hand, my looks are much admired and yet I have not been as successful as her. I would love to know her secret.'

For my part, I had more important secrets to unearth. I began to wonder how such a woman could possibly be involved in a plot to steal the Queen's coronation crown – if indeed she was guilty of anything except having a very sour face! I would have to speak to her myself.

I moved nearer to her. She was standing at a table with bowls of syllabub laid on it. She was in the company of some of the other Dutch women. I was just helping myself to some when I heard something very interesting. Lady Ann Courtenay, one of the Queen's Ladies-in-Waiting, came up to her and laid a hand on her arm.

'Are you feeling better now, Juliana?' she asked kindly. 'I was most worried when I heard you had fainted. I wondered if the armoury store was too close and stuffy. I expect there were many people there.'

'On the contrary,' said Juliana rather stiffly. 'It was a cold place. I was tired of standing; that is all.'

Lady Ann gave a curtsy and moved on. Faith, the Dutch woman was rude. I could not let that put me off, however. This supposed faint – which happened in the very room where the jewels were – could have been a distraction to allow someone to put the laudanum in the guards' beer. In great excitement I gulped down my syllabub and stepped boldly up to her. I noticed that she wore a very fine pendant around her neck. That would be a good starting point.

'Pray excuse my impertinence, my lady,' I said politely, 'but I could not help noticing your wonderful pendant. Can you tell me where it came from?'

The woman looked at me as if I were an ant crawling round her feet. (I had a fleeting thought that I should go and see the Queen's dogs next. At least *they* would be pleased to see me! No one else seemed to be.) She fingered the chain.

'You will not find a piece as splendid as this in England. My husband had it made by the best goldsmith he could find.' She spoke haughtily and turned as if to dismiss me. But I was not to be shaken off so easily.

'Then your husband has exquisite taste,' I sighed. 'It must have been hard to find anything to match your beauty.'

This was rather bold. Juliana is a plain, heavily built woman, but she took it as a compliment.

'Hans would go to the ends of the earth for me,' she said proudly.

I saw one of her group roll her eyes at this. I guessed they must be sick of hearing about the wonderful Hans.

'I have only to speak the word,' she went on. 'Just now he is gone in search of a posset, for I cannot eat this English food.'

I was tempted to say that she looked as if she had eaten enough already! But I kept my counsel.

Instead, I exclaimed, 'Then you are so blessed that the Queen herself would envy you!' Juliana smirked. 'What would Her Majesty give to have

such a husband . . . ?' I pretended to cast about for inspiration. 'Perhaps even her crown jewels.'

I was hoping to get a reaction and she did not disappoint.

A dark shadow immediately passed over Juliana's face. '*Her* crown jewels!' she spat. 'Those jewels that you English are so proud of – they were got by piracy. Your Queen sends her plundering ships onto the high seas to take what they will!' Her heavily ringed fingers flashed in front of my face as she spoke.

My blood boiled. I could not let the woman get away with that, suspect or no suspect! 'Forgive me, my lady,' I said smoothly, struggling to keep my temper down, 'but I fear you have been misinformed. Her Majesty's crown jewels have belonged to the English monarchy for many generations. One is at least five hundred years old – the crown of St Edward that the Queen will wear tomorrow.'

As soon as I had spoken I wished I had not. Suppose the crown is not recovered by tomorrow!

At these words Juliana tottered a little and wiped her brow. 'I am faint again,' she said breathlessly. (More likely suffering from being bested by an

English Maid of Honour!) 'I must go to my chamber immediately. Where is my husband? He must order the Queen's physician to attend me.'

I made a mental note of that. If my Uncle Cavendish were indeed to be called to her bedside, I would be able to find out from him whether the woman was truly ill or not. At least, I would if he was sober! My uncle is quite fond of his wine and it can affect his senses.

One of Juliana's companions took her arm and led her over to the Queen to ask if she might retire. As the question was put, I noticed a curious thing. Her Majesty looked to Mr Hatton for his approval before she gave her permission! He nodded and Juliana made stumbling curtsies backwards out of the Banqueting House as if she might drop at any moment. I watched her all the while: as soon as she got to the door where she thought no one was watching, she shook off her companion and walked quite normally. Well, not quite normally. She had a peculiarly stiff gait. I wondered for a moment if, even now, she was hiding the crown under her vast skirts! Then I concluded it was because she walked with her nose so high in the air.

In any case, her behaviour had been very suspicious – especially when I mentioned the crown of St Edward! I would have to investigate further. And I was also burning to know why the Queen had deferred to Mr Hatton.

Maybe the Captain of the Guard wanted to interrogate Juliana himself. I hoped not. Mr Hatton is never the most delicate of investigators and could frighten off any guilty suspect. Although I admit that I had not been as skilled as I might in my own questioning!

Well, how dare the woman insult Her Majesty in that way – piracy indeed! It is true that – *sometimes* – Spanish treasure ships are captured by sailors such as Captain Francis Drake and his like. They may be known as the Sea Dogs, but they are just being loyal to the Queen. Mistress – or should I say Mevrouw – Juliana should remember that her own Dutchmen do the same – except they are known as the Sea Beggars and are happy to fill their coffers with as much Spanish gold as their ships can bear without sinking.

I suddenly saw that the Queen was leaving the Banqueting House and rushed to attend her, as was my duty. As soon as we had all finished bowing and curtsying, I dodged through the crowds – which was not easy, we were so tightly packed in – and slipped out of the door after her. I saw her

disappearing down a passageway, deep in conversation with some of her advisers, so I hurried round the corner, skidded and collided with Secretary Cecil. He looked at me with great disapproval. (He is a grave man and did not see the funny side at all.)

I muttered an apology, curtsied to the Queen and begged a private word with her. She dismissed her ministers immediately. I felt rather guilty, for I saw a flicker of hope in her eyes. I am sure she thought I was bringing her news of her crown.

'Well, Grace,' she said eagerly, as soon as they were out of earshot. 'What have you discovered? Have you found my crown?' She looked keenly at my face. 'No, I see from your expression that you have not.'

I would have given anything to be able to put the crown of St Edward into her hands. 'I have much to find out before I can bring Your Majesty a solution to this mystery,' I told her gently. 'But I believe the thief to be among us still and I will do my utmost to track him down before he has the chance to humiliate you.' I did not mention the lady from the Low Countries, for I had no proof of any misdeed yet – unless rudeness was a crime, which it ought to be.

The Queen's eyes narrowed. 'I do not share your hope that the crown is still at Court,' she said bitterly. 'If I were the blackguard who took it – curse him – I would have fled Placentia the instant I had my prize. I would not risk my neck playing ransom games!'

I don't know what the thief intended, but he was clever enough to render powerless the monarch of the greatest country in the world! No mean feat!

'So what do you want to tell me?' The Queen sighed.

I do not think I have ever felt more downcast. Her Majesty, my beloved godmother, is usually so strong and determined. Now she seemed to have given up the fight. She looked pale and weary. It frightened me – but it also made me even more determined to take this burden from her if I could.

'My Liege,' I said, 'I saw you defer to Mr Hatton just now when the lady who was faint asked to retire. I wondered . . .'

I saw a slight smile play round the Queen's lips.

'Ah, Grace,' she said. 'You have gladdened my soul. How can my Lady Pursuivant fail to find the thief when her eyes miss nothing?'

I smiled back. But I wondered if she was trying to convince herself.

The Queen explained: 'My good Captain of the Guard had ordered some of his men to search the chambers of all the guests. I was simply making sure that they had finished their task before the end of the celebration. It would not do for word to go round that we do not trust those we ask here to share our celebrations.'

I opened my mouth to speak.

'And to save you the trouble of asking – nothing was discovered.' The Queen's shoulders drooped again. 'I am depending upon *you*, Grace,' she said gravely. 'The crown *must* be found.'

I knelt in front of her. 'I would journey to the sun if it would bring the crown back to my Queen,' I told her.

I knew I must not fail – but how was I to solve this mystery?

Mary has just come in to remind me that I should be in the Great Hall, where we are to have more entertainment from Mr Somers's troupe. I must go! Mayhap I shall find out more about Mistress Juliana from my Uncle Cavendish – if he is there, and sober enough. I will take my daybooke and penner with me, for I do not know how long we will be away. I hope that events will have moved on and I will have something to write.

The Queen's Privy Chamber – three has long since struck

I am sitting in the Queen's Privy Chamber and it is not crowded for a change. The Court and the visitors are still in the Great Hall and the Queen is in her bedchamber.

As soon as we got to the Great Hall, I searched in vain for my Uncle Cavendish. I began to think he was not in the audience. He is often absent, sending the message that he is tired or indisposed. I know what that means – and so do the servants who have to clear away all his empty wine casks!

Then I spotted him coming into the Great Hall – and walking quite steadily! I went to greet him.

'Grace, my dear niece,' he exclaimed with pleasure as soon as he saw me. 'I have not seen you since we arrived at Placentia!'

I did not remark that this was because he preferred the company of drink to the company of the Court. And anyway, I am fond of my uncle, and would not want to wound him with words – even true ones.

'There has been so much to do in preparation for tomorrow, Uncle,' I said. 'Her Majesty wants us all to be at our finest for her celebrations.'

'Phah!' He made a disapproving face. 'Could we not celebrate without the whole of Europe here?'

My uncle is a loyal servant of the Queen and knows as well as I do how important it is to put on a show of might to the world, but he does not relish society. However, he had given me the chance to find out what I wanted to know.

'I believe you had to attend one of Her Majesty's foreign guests who was faint,' I said. 'How irksome that must have been for you.'

'Indeed so,' he said. 'A waste of my time. I was called from my, er, studies for nothing. Far from being faint, the lady had no symptoms of anything that I could discern.'

It was just as I had thought, but my uncle had not finished.

'She told me that I must give her a supply of laudanum, for hers had all gone. You would have thought she was royalty itself, the way she spoke to me.'

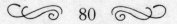

My uncle went on complaining, but I was scarcely listening. Juliana had asked for laudanum because she had used up her supply! Had she used it up drugging the guards' drink?

I thought hard about the theft. If Mistress Juliana was indeed the thief, how had she actually stolen the crown? The Jewel Master was the last to leave the store when he came to see the entertainment. After that, the guards had been overcome by the drug. What then? I could not work it out. I knew that Ellie would have been whispering witchcraft by now, but I am not going to start thinking about that. This was an earthly crime committed by a human, and I will find him – or her – out.

The note posed a problem. It had been written in poor English, but the stout Dutchwoman spoke our language fluently. I was already convinced that the thief was clever, so she could have done that on purpose to throw us off the scent.

I left my uncle and made for the Queen to tell her what I had found out. But I hesitated. I had to admit that there could be an innocent explanation for the laudanum. I needed to be sure before I accused this woman. Another thorough search of her room might sort out the question for us, for where else could she hide the crown?

 81

There was a stir in the crowd, and in the centre was my suspect! She was on her husband's arm and making a fuss because she did not have anywhere to sit. Well, she should have known that she was not of a high enough status to be given a seat. The benches were reserved for those courtiers closest to the Queen, and for the Ambassadors.

Nevertheless several courtiers seemed to be moving politely to let her sit down, which she did with an imperious air, pulling her husband down next to her. Now I saw that there was an empty place beside her. (Perhaps others had realized what she was like!) I decided to take it. I would not have a good view of Masou's acrobatics from there, but it could not be helped if I were to tease more information out of Juliana.

Then I saw that Jane was making for the same seat. I set off as quickly as I could – without looking unseemly. I had just begged the pardon of the third person whose toes I had trodden on, when Jane sat herself down on the bench in a very determined manner. I was so annoyed I wanted to push her off!

My chance of talking to the Dutchwoman might be lost for hours if Jane had her way – and I did not have the luxury of time in which to solve this mystery! I hovered nearby, pretending to pick at some sort of imperfection on my gown while I eavesdropped.

Jane was set on striking up a conversation with the haughty Hollander. She began by asking Mistress Juliana for advice about fashions! Considering that the woman looked like a brightly painted ship under full sail, I did not think Jane could be serious. But the two of them were soon discussing all the latest gown and hat and glove styles.

I found myself puzzled as to why Jane should be at all interested in Juliana. Then I remembered her remark when she found out that the lady had a very wealthy husband. She wanted to know how to capture one for herself. I resigned myself to standing behind their chairs and awaiting my opportunity to pipe up. But neither of them drew breath!

'A year ago,' Jane was now saying to her companion, 'one of your wonderful noblemen taught us to skate on the frozen Thames. What a feeling it was to glide effortlessly up and down – and all thanks to his tutoring. I have felt very close to the people of the Low Countries since then.'

I let out a snort at hearing this – which I hurriedly pretended was a sneeze. Jane has made absolutely no mention of the Hollanders from that time to this. I recalled that she spent most of her time on her bottom rather than skating. Her words were obviously just to gain the lady's interest.

Their conversation was halted by the arrival of the troupe. They did some fine whirling cartwheels around the small space allowed them in the crush. Then they formed a tall pyramid. Masou stood on the top, perfectly poised as usual. Mr Somers announced that he would do a double somersault backwards and land on French Louis's shoulders. I did not envy French Louis! Everyone gasped and fell silent. But suddenly there was a great rumbling noise from just in front of me. Juliana's husband was snoring!

The whole pyramid glared at him. Mr Somers announced Masou again as if nothing had happened. Masou prepared to jump – and nearly fell off the pyramid as another loud snore burst out. He put his hands on his hips and looked furiously at the offending snorer. (I think he would have stamped his foot if he hadn't been balanced on Peter and Paul's shoulders.) Some of the audience began to laugh – perhaps they thought it was part of the entertainment. Mistress Juliana gave her husband a dig in the ribs and the snores subsided.

Little Gypsy Pete gave a dramatic roll on the drum and Masou sprang high in the air. I caught my breath – I always have a moment of fear when my friend does his daring feats. He tucked himself into a ball, spun over and over and landed light as a feather on French Louis's shoulders. I clapped until my hands nearly dropped off. It was breathtaking. (But I must remember to tease him about making his audience nod off. It is not often that I have the pleasure of deflating his usually swollen head!)

As the whole troupe lined up for their final applause, Juliana's husband suddenly woke up with a snort and got to his feet. He bowed to Jane, said a word in his wife's ear and stumbled off towards the Queen. Mistress Juliana leaned across to Jane. 'My husband is feeling a little unwell,' she explained. 'He is hoping to retire to our chamber if your Queen allows.'

In other words, he wants to go and have a proper sleep where he won't be dug in the ribs every few minutes, I thought to myself.

'It is all very well marrying a rich husband,' Juliana went on bitterly, 'but sometimes things are not what they first appear.'

What could she mean? Had her husband claimed to be rich but then she had found out, too late, that

he was lying? I was soon to learn the truth.

Juliana pursed her lips in disdain as she watched her husband leave the Great Hall. 'He gives me everything I ask for – but one thing. A quiet night's sleep! He is a snorer.'

Jane nodded sympathetically.

'I share my bed with a trumpet,' her new friend continued. 'The only answer is laudanum. I take a dose before retiring so that I may sleep through it – and I would advise you to do so if you get a husband who is thus afflicted.'

Poor Jane! Was this the best marriage advice the woman had for her? I could imagine her quizzing each prospective husband to find out if they snored!

However, for the mystery at hand, it seemed the laudanum might have an innocent explanation. But I had to be sure. She could still have used some of it for a wicked purpose.

Suddenly I realized I was being spoken to.

'Grace!' Jane tugged on my sleeve. 'Mistress Juliana is kindly giving some advice that you would do well to follow.'

I forced my face into a smile as the Hollander looked me up and down critically.

'Your colours are wrong,' she told me bluntly. 'You will never be noticed if you wear such pale

tones. You need reds, yellows and gold if you wish to attract a suitable husband.'

I was highly insulted – on Ellie's behalf more than my own, for she had chosen the gown I was wearing. 'I thank you, madam,' I said coldly. 'But I have the services of an expert in matters of dress. And I have no intention – or need – of marrying for money, or indeed at all!'

Juliana looked at me as if I had grown a second nose. Then she snapped her head away, rose with a derisive sniff and stalked off.

Jane rounded on me. 'How dare you offend one of Her Majesty's guests!' she hissed. 'Especially when she was merely giving you some well-meant advice. You would do well to listen, Grace. I stood with her during the whole of the entertainment this morning and she was wonderfully helpful. I shall be ordering new cloth directly.' Her eyes sparkled. 'And who knows what effect it will have on the men of the Court.'

I was about to retort that people would believe Jane to be part of Mr Somers's troupe if she dressed in such garish colours. Then I suddenly realized that she had unwittingly proved Juliana innocent of the theft. If the Hollander had been with Jane all the time, she could not have stolen the crown. The faint in the armoury was no longer entirely suspicious – lack of sleep could have been the cause – and she had an innocent reason for wanting the laudanum. Now I saw her for what she really was – a spoiled, empty-headed woman who was so obsessed with riches that she could not keep away from the crown jewels.

And, unfortunately, she could be not be arrested for that.

But at least Jane had saved me from the embarrassment of going to the Queen with a false accusation. It would not do to shatter her hopes again this day. I could only pray that Mr Hatton, for once, was faring better in his own investigation. I was completely without a suspect now. Was this going to be the first mystery to defeat Her Majesty's Lady Pursuivant? This could not happen! Especially now the Queen had implored me to act. I would ferret out the crown or die in the attempt. (I was feeling particularly dramatic at that moment.)

'Grace!' It was Jane. 'Great Heavens! You are in a dream again. We are called to attend Her Majesty.'

God's Oath! I thought to myself – more delays before I can be about my work. Jane dragged me along to where the Queen sat on her salamander chair, surrounded by all the foreign dignitaries, who were trying to outdo each other in their strange flatteries. How does Her Majesty put up with such nonsense? She must know that each of them just wants her to form a marriage alliance with his own country. One Spanish gentleman was comparing her with some sort of fish! When the Queen looked a little startled, he hurriedly explained that this was the highest compliment where he came from, as eating the fish in question was known to bring good luck.

'This is one fish that is not so easily caught!' exclaimed Her Majesty, and everyone laughed. But they all knew what she meant. She was not going to let herself be married off until *she* decided it was time – which I hope is never! I also hoped that such a statement from the Queen would put an end to the constant gossip about her plans for marriage, but I knew this would never happen – whatever else would the Maids and Ladies talk about when anticipating a visit from a foreign party?

I took my seat on a cushion at her side, cursing inwardly that I could not continue my investigations and might not get the chance for some hours. My eyes fell on the Queen's carved chair and I only just stopped myself jumping up in surprise. Something was tucked behind one of the carved golden vine leaves. It was a small scroll of the same paper as the first note from the thief. I shuffled on my cushion to get closer. Everyone's eyes were on the Queen, as ever, so it was simple task to pull the scroll out.

While the assembled Ambassadors were guffawing over another of Her Majesty's clever remarks, I took a very quick look at it – just long enough to see, with a start, that it was written in the same untidy hand as before. The thief had struck again. My heartbeat quickened. What did it say? I could not risk reading it in public. I had to speak to the Queen and persuade her to withdraw to somewhere private to read it.

I stood up and smoothed out my gown. I was trembling with excitement and dread. Her Majesty turned to me and I thought she was going to chide me for fidgeting. But she must have seen something in my face for she looked questioningly into my eyes. I found my mouth was dry as I bent forward to her, and my excited whisper came out as a squeak!

'Another note, Your Majesty!' was all I managed as I secretly pressed the scroll into her hand.

The Queen said nothing in reply, but her knuckles were white as she crushed the scroll

between her fingers. She stood quickly, taking everyone by surprise. The whole Court bowed low. Of course, the Ladies-in-Waiting and Maids hurriedly got up from their cushions to follow, but the Queen dismissed them with an impatient flap of her hand.

'Stay there,' she ordered. 'I would have Secretary Cecil accompany me to my Privy Chamber, for I must needs dictate a letter. And Mr Hatton – I will take your arm. I find myself somewhat weary.' What a fine play actor the Queen would be! Anyone would think she had chosen the Captain of the Guard at random. Only I knew that he must see the note too. As she swept to the door, the Queen gave me a stare and a little nod. She wanted me to follow.

That was all very well, but I could not just run out after her! Mrs Champernowne would have something to say about that. I had to contrive some way of leaving the Great Hall. Then I had it. Mrs Champernowne was heading my way – no doubt to get me back safely onto my cushion again. I picked up my daybooke, then dived down and pretended to pick up something from the rushes on the floor.

'What do you think you are at, Grace,' said the

Mistress of the Maids, 'scrapping about down there like a common urchin?'

'But, Mrs Champernowne,' I said, inventing like mad, 'I spotted a row of pearls falling from Her Majesty's gown as she left.' I held my hand in a fist as if the pearls were in there. 'I will take them to her straight away.'

'You will do no such thing,' Mrs Champernowne huffed. 'The Queen would be most angry if you disturbed her now. I will see that they are returned to her.' She held out her hand for them. I felt my chest tighten in panic. How was I going to get out of this?

I kept my fist tightly closed. 'But if I try to give them to you, I will certainly spill them and they will be lost for ever!' I told her. 'And she will be even more angry when she finds they're gone.'

'Nonsense, child!' she exclaimed.

'I happen to know . . .' I went on, thinking desperately, 'that . . . that . . . they were given to her by the Earl of Leicester! I really must not delay in returning them.'

And before Mrs Champernowne could protest further, I made my escape. I wonder if Lord Robert has ever given the Queen any pearls. I am sure he has, for they are her favourite jewel – and she is his favourite person – so I could have been right. I also wonder if Mrs Champernowne will chide me for my defiance when she catches up with me.

The guards outside the Privy Chamber were astonished when I ran up and rapped loudly on the door. My knock was answered by a bellow from the Queen.

'Who dares disturb my peace?'

I knew that the Queen would have to act as if I was the last person she wanted to see – and yet I still felt a little tightening in my belly. Her Majesty can be so fierce.

'Rather you than me, my lady,' muttered one of the guards as I opened the door.

I dropped to the floor in a deep curtsy while the Queen threw the necessary insults at me to keep up our pretence. I am glad she threw nothing harder!

'I will not even ask what you are come for, you brainless codfish,' she finished. 'But here you will stay until my business is finished.'

She turned to Mr Hatton, who might have protested at my presence had he got the chance. 'It is better for the silly girl to sit here bored than to be engaged in idle gossip with the other Maids,' she said. 'I must take my god-daughter in hand, do you not think, gentlemen? Although, by the look of her, it is already too late.'

I was annoyed to see Mr Hatton nodding in vigorous agreement! (Although part of me wanted to smile. Long may he think me a fool. It makes my investigations easier.)

'Now sit in the corner and do not make mischief,' said the Queen. 'There are plenty of Latin texts on my table for you to read. Be sure you attend *most closely* to each word.'

I hope I did not show anything in my face at this. It always gives me a warm feeling inside when the Queen speaks in a code that only I understand. I would indeed attend 'most closely', but not to any Latin text!

'Just as Your Majesty wishes,' I said demurely and withdrew to the corner with a book of Ovid's poems.

I gave every appearance of studying the lines intently, holding the book up so that I could peek over it. The Queen now turned her attention to her Secretary and Captain of the Guard.

'The thief has dared to leave me another note!' she thundered, thrusting the scroll into Mr Hatton's hand. Despite the mystery still being unsolved, I was actually rather pleased to see that the Queen's eyes were flashing – the villain's audacity had brought the fight back into her.

'Your Majesty,' murmured Secretary Cecil. 'Should we lower our voices? The guards outside . . .' He is one of the few people at Court who would ever dare to tell the Queen to keep her voice down and even he looked nervous!

'Those two guards have knowledge of the theft, William,' snapped the Queen. 'Do you think I would be so foolish as to let our dreadful secret out?'

Secretary Cecil bowed his head.

'Read the note, Mr Hatton,' Her Majesty ordered. 'I would not deign to look at it when I found it, knowing the thief could be watching me and glorying in my anger.'

The Captain of the Guard hesitated. 'May I advise you to dismiss Lady Grace?' he said quietly. 'These matters are not for her ears.'

'Do not be foolish, man!' shouted the Queen, bringing her fist down on the table. 'I will wait no longer to hear what new degradations await me – and she is not the brightest star in the heavens. It will go over her head.'

It is a very good thing I know just how much Her Majesty loves me – otherwise I might wonder how she manages to have a brand-new insult for me every time one is needed!

Mr Hatton began to read the note in a voice so low that I could scarcely hear him. I cleared my throat. Mercifully my signal was not lost on Her Majesty.

'Do not mumble into your beard, man!' she told him immediately. 'Speak up!'

'*I wish a cart pulled by a . . . horse that is fast and strong,*' read Mr Hatton, stumbling over some of the scrawled words. '*The cart filled with gold. The Queen of England she hand the . . . reins to me under the Conduit Court clock when it will be striking the seven. She must not fail . . . or she never is seeing her crown again.*'

The Queen was white with anger. 'How dare this man make bargains with us!' She paced about the room, her gown swishing. 'But I *will* have my crown back. I have vowed to wear it tomorrow – and wear it I shall!'

How could the thief think he would get away in a cart carrying a heavy load – and from one of the inner courtyards of the palace? Was he just mocking her? My heart leaped into my mouth. He surely wasn't this foolish. He must have had another plan in mind, from which he was hoping to distract the

Queen with this note. But what could it be? Was he going to kill her? It would not be the first time an attempt has been made on her life. Surely she could not be contemplating meeting this dangerous thief. I yearned to leap up and shout, 'No, Your Majesty!' Instead I bit my lip hard. I had to go on pretending I had heard nothing. But I vowed to try to find the thief before seven struck.

'My Liege, you will, of course, refuse this demand,' said Secretary Cecil gravely. 'Who knows what the demon has planned for you the minute you make the exchange?'

I prayed Her Majesty would listen to his wise words.

'Do you counsel the Queen of England to baulk at such a challenge?' she demanded scornfully. 'I shall be in the Conduit Court when the clock strikes seven. I fear nothing for my own safety. My guards will be stationed all around and will kill the coward the very instant he appears. Mr Hatton – you will see to it. And that, gentlemen, will be an end to the matter.'

Mr Hatton nodded approvingly – he always prefers the path of action – but Secretary Cecil still looked worried.

'If I cannot sway Your Majesty from this

hazardous course,' he said, 'I advise you to wear full armour.'

'I may be bold, but I am not foolhardly,' the Queen told him tersely. 'And now away with you both. I have had enough of talk.'

Mr Hatton and Secretary Cecil could do nothing but bow low and back away. The moment the door closed behind them I put down my Ovid and jumped to my feet, my heart pounding with fear. I began to plead with the Queen not to carry out this reckless plan.

'Your Majesty, I beg you not to—'

'Do not try to sway my course,' said the Queen. 'You have done all you can, Grace, but I believe that your investigations may be over now. I shall retire to my bedchamber. Until I meet the villain and have the crown of St Edward in my hands again, I would be alone.'

When she had gone I snatched up my daybooke and penner to write down all that had taken place. Well, I trust I have remembered 'every word', as the Queen instructed, even if she now thinks I am no longer needed!

I know I will become more and more fearful for the Queen as seven o'clock draws nearer. I must do all I can to prevent her going out to meet the thief

– this means that I must either catch the blackguard or find the crown before seven o'clock tonight.

I have decided my only possible next step is to speak to the guards who were drugged as they guarded the jewels. I pray they are awake and remember something.

Five of the clock, only two hours until the Conduit Clock strikes seven

I fear my hand will drop off at any moment. I have written so much today and still have much more to put down. I am in my bedchamber and Ellie is attending to my hair. I have had a little tussle with a rose bush, and although I would have just tucked the loose tendrils behind my ears, Mrs Champernowne caught me and had a blue fit. However, this suits my purpose, for I can catch up with events since my last entry. I just hope I can get everything down – having told Ellie about the taunting note left to Her Majesty, she has been constantly muttering oaths to herself that can be rather distracting. She seems more outraged at the thief's taunting of Her Majesty than the Queen herself!

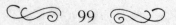

★ ★ ★

When I emerged from the Privy Chamber I had less than three hours to continue with my investigations before the Queen went to her perilous meeting. I was desperate to talk with the two Tower guards and find out what they knew, and here was my chance. I went to my chamber and summoned Ellie. It would be unseemly if I approached them unchaperoned but with my tiring woman I could feign any number of errands. And I wanted my friend with me.

Ellie was quick to arrive. 'I've seen all sorts of fashions; you wouldn't believe, Grace,' she said, eyes bright. 'Them Frenchies know how to style a skirt and—'

Closing the door, I quickly told her about the drugged guards and the missing crown. Of course, the Queen had forbidden talk of this, but Mr Hatton had been allowed to confide in his most faithful men so I, as Lady Pursuivant, could surely confide in a trusted companion of my own. I would certainly need Ellie's help (Masou's too, I warrant).

'No!' Ellie was shocked at my news. 'Who would do such an evil thing?' She looked wildly around the room. 'One of them foreigners, I'll be bound.

How can they be trusted when they don't even speak the Queen's English!'

I laughed. 'That would not get them very far in their own country. And you will be claiming they have tails next, just like Mrs Fadget used to tell you when you worked in the laundry!'

She opened her mouth – to protest or agree, I know not which.

'But you have the right of one thing,' I said quickly. 'It is most likely one of the visitors who has done this, intent on ruining our Queen's reputation. We need to speak to the Tower guards, if they have awakened from their drugged sleep.'

'Come on then,' declared Ellie, going to the door. 'What are you waiting for?'

But I had to tell her where the men were resting and I did not think I would find her so eager once she knew this.

'They are in the guardroom by the Palace Gate,' I told her.

Ellie went white. 'Oh no, Grace,' she whispered. 'You can't make me go there.'

Poor Ellie never went near the Palace Gate. Only last year she had been falsely accused of theft and held prisoner in the little cell there. She did not like to talk about it.

'I cannot go alone,' I pleaded. 'And the Queen is depending on us.'

'I can't,' said Ellie in a wobbly voice. 'It just reminds me of how dark and cold it was, and how scared I got. I thought I was going to have my hand cut off.'

'Then do not worry yourself any longer,' I said, with a scheme brewing in my mind. I did not want to take her where she feared to go, but this was in the service of Her Majesty. 'I will disguise myself as a laundrymaid, and then no one will question my actions if I am alone. I just 'ave to tawk loike a servant and bob me 'ead when I sees a nobbleman!'

Ellie burst out laughing. 'You'll more like be put in Bedlam with that speech!' She stood up straight. 'I'll come with you,' she declared bravely.

'Thank you, Ellie.' I gave her a big hug. 'Where would I be without you?' A look of mischief crossed her face and she laughed. 'No, do not tell me!'

I lent her one of my cloaks and, warmly wrapped, we went across the gardens to the Palace Gate. Ellie seemed to hold back at the sight of the guardhouse, so I took her hand and led her in.

Mr Morling stood by the inner door. 'What business have you here, Lady Grace?' he asked.

God's teeth! I should have realized that Mr Hatton would put a man to watch over the guards! The thief might think them a threat. He would have no idea if they had seen anything and might seek to stop their mouths if he knew they were awake.

'I am sent by . . . Mrs Champernowne,' I said in a rush. 'She thought the men might be in need of a restorative posset and we are the only ones to know they are here.' I felt a flutter of pride at how quickly I could think on my feet these days. The pride faded away like melted snow when I realized that I held no such posset in my hands.

'So we are to ask them if they need one.' Clever Ellie had seen my dilemma and came to my rescue.

'I would not like to displease the Mistress of the Maids by returning with no answer,' I said, fluttering my eyelashes.

'Of course not,' said Mr Morling gallantly. 'They have just begun to wake, and I have sent a messenger to get Mr Hatton.' He stepped aside and let us into the inner guardroom.

'We must be gone from here before Mr Hatton arrives,' I whispered to Ellie.

The Tower guards were sitting by the fire. They struggled to keep their eyes open in the warmth, so they must still have been feeling the effects of the laudanum. There was no one else there, which I was glad of. Mr Hatton had his men busy. The rest of the jewels had gone back to the Tower and the Queen had insisted on a large escort of men.

I was glad that they were still very drowsy, for I hoped they would not remember much of what I asked when they were fully awake again. But it was hard to keep their attention as they sat, eyelids drooping and heads nodding.

'Mrs Champernowne sent me to ask how you were,' I said. 'On behalf of the Queen.'

'Doing nicely, thank you, my lady,' said one, slurring his words a little. The other just grinned stupidly. I put it down to the drug. The Tower guards are normally alert, bright men and he was the one who had spoken to me earlier when the jewels first arrived. He had not appeared half-witted then.

'Do you remember what happened?' I decided to be direct. I had no idea how long they would stay awake and whether someone else might come along.

'Not a thing.' The guard gave a huge yawn. 'Begging your pardon, my lady. Mr Bennett said there wouldn't be any visitors for a while, so John and I could take a tankard of small beer. It had been a long morning. And we didn't expect any trouble. Not with Mr Hatton's men outside. And the next thing I knew we were waking up here.'

I wondered what I was going to have to do to glean any more information, and quickly, before Hatton showed up. Then the other guard spoke, as if in his sleep.

'The crown . . . !'

I rushed to his side. 'What about the crown?' I demanded.

'It floated through the air . . .'

But then he began to snore deeply and did not wake even when I pinched him. (Which was a little unkind, I admit.)

I asked the other guard, who shrugged. 'I cannot recall, I'm afraid.'

I wanted to stay and ask more questions – or shake the sleeping guard awake – but Ellie pulled at my sleeve. 'Hatton'll be here at any moment!' she said.

We had no choice but to leave.

'What did he mean by floating?' I wondered aloud.

'Nothing,' snorted Ellie. 'It were the laudanum talking, that's all. It does that to a brain. Don't you remember when Lady Sarah got badly burned and had to have it for the pain? She told you she had all sorts of strange dreams.'

'You may be right,' I murmured. 'But I will discount nothing. I want another look at the storeroom, and now would be a perfect time. The jewels are gone so there will be no guards.'

There were footsteps outside and it sent my heart racing. What would Hatton think if he saw me here? But it was the Jewel Master who came in. He started in surprise. Obviously two young ladies in velvet cloaks were the last people he expected to see.

'Good day, Mr Bennett,' I said boldly. 'The Queen sent me to see how the men were faring after their ordeal.'

I was again pleased with my quick thinking. He would never dare ask Her Majesty if that were true. I doubted the men would remember that it had been Mrs Champernowne in my first explanation. Mr Bennett nodded and went into the guardroom.

Ellie and I set off through the gardens towards the armoury, relieved that we had escaped before Hatton arrived. We walked briskly, for the sun had long gone and it was very cold. When we reached the passage that led to the storeroom, there was not a guard in sight.

The room seemed a little forlorn now, with the jewels gone. The table was still there, but the cloth was crooked. One torch gave a meagre light. The flagon of small beer had been taken away – to stop anyone else being drugged – and the little stool it had been resting on was lying on its side.

'What do you think happened, Grace?' asked Ellie, looking about her. 'How did that rascally cur get in 'ere?'

'There is only one door and no windows,' I said.

And all of sudden, a realization came to me – just because a room looked as if it offered no escape did not mean that the escape was not concealed. In my time as Lady Pursuivant, I had seen acrobatic thieves, hidden weapons and secret rooms.

'We have been fooled by secret rooms before, Ellie,' I said. 'We need to test *these* walls to make sure that there is no other way the crown could have been snuck out.'

We made our way round, tapping on the whitewash; it was a task soon done.

'Nothing here,' declared Ellie.

'There has to be *something*,' I said crossly. 'The crown could not disappear by magic.' I saw a look of fear cross her face. 'No it could *not*, Ellie. There has to be an answer. Where else could the thief have got in if not by the door or through the wall?'

'But you've said it yourself, Grace,' insisted Ellie. 'There's no way in except for that door and it was guarded by Mr Westerland – a loyal servant of Her Majesty, with nineteen others just like him close by.' She wrung her hands. 'I wish I'd thought to bring an amulet with me against bad spirits.'

I looked at the table in the dimly lit room, trying to imagine the jewels there. And then I remembered what the drowsy Tower guard had said. *A floating crown.* How could that be? Perhaps Ellie was right and it had just been the words of someone dreaming. Yet I had no other clues to work with. However impossible it seemed, I decided to pursue it for now. Feeling a little foolish, I tried to imagine what path a flying crown might have taken. I crouched down where the guard had been lying and looked up.

I studied the carved design of sun and moon on the ceiling. Nothing there. No, wait! That wasn't true . . .

'Look at that sunbeam, Ellie!' I gasped. 'That's how the crown left the room.'

Poor Ellie looked at me as if I were mazed. 'What are you on about, Grace?'

I pointed up at the panel that had one of the rays of sunlight on it.

'See the painted sunbeam up there?' I said, trying not to squeak in excitement. 'It is not aligned properly. Someone has removed one of the panels and put it back a little crooked.'

'So that's how the thief got in and out,' said Ellie, gazing up at the offending panel. 'But how did he reach the crown without a ladder? Did he fly?' She looked worried again.

'The guard only mentioned a *crown* floating, not a person,' I said. 'But a crown cannot move on its own, let alone float in the air.' The villain could not have manoeuvred the crown up and out of the room, unless he had arms as long as ropes. Or a rope . . . Or . . .

And then I remembered the courtiers fishing early this morning. 'Of course!' I yelled, making Ellie jump. 'The thief used a fishing line.' I stood by the table. 'The crown was here and the panel is almost directly above. The thief could have come in with a group of guests to inspect the jewels and seen that the ceiling was panelled and mayhap he could work one loose. That done, it would be easy to lower a line and hook the crown up. The guard was not dreaming. He saw it float!'

The thief was clever indeed. He would have had to devise this plan very quickly as no one knew the crown would be here until this morning. It was exciting to have solved the manner of the crime, but I was still no closer to knowing who the criminal was.

I had to follow the trail and hope further clues would present themselves. I had to get up onto the roof and check that panel for myself. It would be precarious up there and I would need someone who was skilled in balancing – my dear friend Masou.

A moment later

I dropped my quill because Ellie just gave an extra hard tug at a tangle in my hair! Fortunately, I stained neither paper nor myself.

We found Masou in the Glass Gallery, where he and the troupe were entertaining the foreign guests. Our friend was juggling seven walnuts in front of a group of French visitors. They were clearly impressed when Gypsy Pete threw another nut to him and he deftly spun eight above his head. It was a shame to break this up but I needed my friend and we had little time. Of course, I could not speak to him directly – that would not be fitting.

'You will have to pretend there's some message for him,' I whispered to Ellie.

'What on God's earth am I going to say?' she whispered back.

'I do not know – something about him being needed somewhere,' I hissed. 'Go on!'

Ellie went up and stood by his elbow. I could see she was putting Masou off because after a few more turns he caught all the walnuts and bowed to his audience. She whispered in his ear and he tossed the nuts to Gypsy Pete and hurried away with her. I met up with them outside the gallery.

'From one bunch of nuts to another!' He grinned. 'You must have important business indeed, to take me from mine.'

'I am afraid so,' I said and told him all about the theft.

'By Shaitan!' he growled. 'That is devilish business indeed.'

'I believe that the thief fished the crown up

through the ceiling,' I said. 'So will you take me up onto the roof?'

'Anything for you, my lady.' Masou gave a bow. 'But first I would like to see the room where the crown was taken from,' he said.

Soon we were back in the storeroom. I pointed out the panel with the crooked sunbeam.

'It does indeed look odd,' said Masou, stroking his chin. 'Let me inspect it more closely.'

He went to the wall and, in a flash, climbed up, using the sconces and tiny imperfections in the brickwork. And here, in the secrecy of my daybooke, I can say how impressed I was with his agility! I will never tell Masou, of course, for he will not be able to balance at the top of a pyramid of tumblers if he has a big head! (Well, bigger than it is already with all the praise he gets!)

'How's he doing that?' gasped Ellie as he scuttled across the ceiling like a spider.

'He's holding onto the beams,' I said.

Masou reached the panel with the ray of sun and pushed on it. 'It is loose,' he called down to us. 'There are tiles above it but I can also see the sky above.'

He let go of the beams and dropped to the ground, turning a somersault as he fell.

'That is a fair height,' he said, stroking his chin and looking thoughtful. I must say, it was rather nice to have him thinking so purposefully – usually, Masou is distracted by teasing us both. 'Indeed, the height makes me doubt your story about a hook and line. How could the thief be so accurate?'

'It *has* to be the method used,' I declared hotly. 'The guard saw the crown float and something like a fishing line is the only answer.'

Masou thought for a moment. Then his eyes widened and he fixed us with a meaningful look. (That didn't take long.) 'Ah, ladies, have I not told you of the fakirs of India who can rise up a rope and disappear into the air?' He waved his fingers. 'I saw them many a time on my travels with my father. Perchance that is the explanation.'

Ellie began to look frightened again.

'Nonsense!' I exclaimed. 'By your own admission, you have never travelled to India, Masou. And crowns cannot climb ropes!'

Ellie swiped at Masou, who dodged with a chuckle.

'Then I can think of no other way but fishing,' he admitted, looking serious once more. 'Though it sounds ridiculous. There must be some other explanation.'

'I'll wager a silver coin that it is a line and hook,' I said.

Masou grinned. 'I accept. I will go up onto the roof and prove you wrong. French Louis likes to catch his supper from the Thames. I will get his line.'

'You are not going up on that roof without me,' I said. 'I want to make sure you give it a fair test to win the money.'

'My money is safe,' said Masou. 'But come by all means – if you think you can stand the height.'

'I will be fine,' I declared bravely. 'Ellie, you stay here and keep watch for us.'

'Gladly,' said Ellie. 'I couldn't go up there. You're both woodwild.'

Then I had a thought. 'We need a crown – or something like it.'

'I know just the thing,' said Ellie. She reached over and grabbed Masou's blue velvet hat. She placed it on the table. 'Not half as grand as a crown' – she grinned – 'nor as heavy, but it should serve.'

It took Masou but a few moments to fetch the line and hook and we made our way into King Henry's towers. They had been built as part of the armouries and gave us easy access to the roof through a large window. That part was easy. But now, to reach the old storeroom, we had to cross two sloping courses of tiles. No easy feat for a Maid of Honour in a fine gown (and it *is* a fine gown regardless of what a sour-faced Hollander might say).

I had not bargained for how cold and slippery the tiles would be. And how dark it was! We were a long way from any torches. One good thing: I could not see the ground. That had nothing to do with me being scared of heights. It was just that if I could not see the ground, I reasoned that no one on the ground could see *us*.

'Bend down,' said Masou, 'and use your hands and feet. That way it will be simpler for you to keep your balance.'

I am lucky to have a good friend who is an expert in these matters and I thanked him for his advice. And then a seed of mischief began to grow in my head.

'You must be losing your touch, Masou,' I said sweetly. 'For that Dutch merchant earlier was so unimpressed by your antics that he fell asleep. Remember his snores?'

'Do not decry my skills,' he retorted. The memory was obviously still sore. 'For without me you would have fallen to your death six tiles ago. So be nice to me, Grace, and you may make it back to Ellie in one piece!'

I was about to tell him that I could manage very well when my foot hit a patch of ice and I slipped and began to slide sideways from the peak of the roof. Masou shot out a hand and grasped mine firmly. He held me in a grip of iron until I was steady again.

'Go ahead and boast,' I said, trying not to let my voice wobble. 'You have earned it this one time.'

'That was nothing,' said Masou with a shrug. 'If you had fallen, I would have jumped down first and been there to catch you.' (He is quite impossible! But also a dear friend.)

At last we reached the roof of the storeroom. The slope of the tiles was not as steep here.

'Look!' I gasped, pointing across to where some tiles had been removed and stacked beside a gaping hole. We made our way to it and Masou reached in and grasped the ceiling panel. He pulled it up and placed it carefully with the tiles. Then he looked down into the room.

'Greetings, fair Ellie,' he called softly.

I knelt beside him and peered down. There she stood by the table, gawping up at us. We must have made quite a picture even though she had been expecting us.

We could see Masou's hat on the table. It was not directly beneath the hole but was not too far away. Masou fed the string through the gap in the roof. At first he made it swing violently and Ellie had to duck out of the way of the hook.

'See' – he chuckled – 'the only thing I am likely to catch is a tiring woman!'

'Do it properly,' I said. 'Or better still, let me.'

'I am only jesting with you, Grace,' said Masou, holding the line still. Now he swung it gently towards his hat. The hook caught on the second attempt and he pulled it up.

'It does look like it's floating,' called Ellie.

The hat came through the gap in the ceiling with plenty of room to spare. Masou disentangled it and stuck it back on his head.

'That is a silver coin you owe me,' I said in triumph. Then I grinned. 'Buy something nice for Ellie instead.'

'I am at your command!' Masou gave a sweeping bow, even though he was balanced on the roof.

I looked around the roof for any clues – a scrap of cloth, anything – but there were none.

We carefully replaced the ceiling panel and the

tiles and then made our way back to the armoury tower. Ellie came running to join us when we emerged at ground level.

'We know how the crown was stolen,' I said. 'But now . . .'

'There is just the small matter of who stole it.' Masou was looking thoughtful again. 'Have you any suspects, Grace?'

'Only every single person at Court!' I retorted. 'I must go now and tell the Queen what I have learned so far. Thank you, my friends.'

Masou skipped away, and Ellie and I were just about to cross the Cellar Court when we heard voices. It was Mr Hatton and Mr Bennett, coming from the Palace Gate guardhouse. I did not want to explain my presence so I ducked behind a thick rose bush, pulling Ellie down beside me.

'They have nothing of use to tell us,' Mr Hatton was saying. 'The thief waited until they were deeply asleep.'

They had not heard of the 'floating crown' or seen the opening in the roof. Or perhaps they *had* heard the ramblings of the guards and disregarded them as nonsense. Well, I would tell the Queen what I had discovered, and she could tell her Captain of the Guard if he could not figure it out for himself. I struggled to stand up from my hiding place after they had gone, and it was then that I caught my hair in the rose briar and got into quite a tangle. As I said, I would not have bothered to do anything about it, but inside the palace we turned a corner and bumped straight into Mrs Champernowne, who shooed me off to get it tidied. I think she compared me to a scarecrow.

So here we are in my chamber. My hair is straight again. I just wish my thoughts were. I know how the crown was stolen but have no idea who the thief is. I do know when the crown was stolen, of course. The theft took place during the morning's entertainment, and this is my only line of inquiry to find the suspect – which I must do before the exchange at seven!

I had to find out if anyone had been missing. I need eager, inquisitive eyes. And I know exactly where to find those – my fellow Maids of Honour.

In the Great Hall, before six

It is just over an hour before the Queen must face the thief in the courtyard. I am sitting in the Great

Hall with my daybooke on my lap. We have been summoned here to listen to the musicians in the gallery. It is not only so that our ears may be regaled with sweet tones that the Queen gave this order. She also does not want anyone near the Conduit Court when the exchange is made. It is imperative that no one ever finds out what befell the crown on this day.

We have just listened to a French motet and now it is a Spanish country song. The performers know how to please their mixed audience. Mary has just informed me that we will be hearing favourites from each of our guests' countries – so that no one will feel left out. That will take a while.

I am finding it hard to sit still, for I have found out something very worrying and am desperate to act upon it. Mrs Champernowne is looking my way, so I must not fidget, even though I long to jump up and get about my business. Instead I have my head bowed over my book and am trying to appear solemn, as if I am writing the most serious of meditations – which, of course, they are. Just not what Mrs Champernowne might be expecting of me. The moment she shifts her beady gaze I will be away.

★ ★ ★

After my last entry, when I joined my fellow Maids in the Great Hall, they were surrounded by a cluster of young men – each of them visitors to our Court. It was most vexing to be taken away from my investigation, but I put on my best smile and hoped to endure.

All manner of flirting was going on – even Mary Shelton looked a little pink in the cheeks as a Venetian gentleman paid her compliments, and she is usually very steady. Lady Sarah did not join in. She looked about as if she were searching for someone. And I knew it was Mr Cheshire she sought. What a change there has been in Sarah! Only a few months ago she would have won prizes for her skill in flirting.

I caught myself looking for her gallant Gentleman Guard on her behalf. I was surprised that Daniel Cheshire was not in close attendance. They are always to be found in each other's company. And indeed Sarah looked a little anxious. I hoped there had not been a lover's tiff between the two.

But that was not getting me further in my purpose. I wanted to find out if anyone had been missing from the morning's entertainment.

'Mary,' I said, grabbing a moment while her

Venetian drew breath. 'How have you been? Faith, it has been so busy here that I have hardly seen you.'

Mary took my hands and pulled me away from the crowd. 'Thank you, Grace,' she whispered. 'I was finding Signor Robbellini a terrible trial. He speaks no English and could be comparing me to a turnip for all I can make out.' She linked arms with me and we joined the throng again.

'I was just telling Mary how much I enjoyed this morning's entertainment,' I said in a loud voice so that all the Maids and their admirers turned. Mary pinched my arm, for of course we had been speaking of nothing of the kind. 'I feel sorry for anyone who did not see the spectacle.'

'Daniel Cheshire missed every moment of it,' sighed Lady Sarah.

This gave me a jolt of surprise. I had not expected to hear that name in response to my cunning remark.

'Perhaps he had duties,' I said, hoping that she would tell me he had.

'He has certainly been very busy lately,' said Sarah with a pout. 'He told me he could not stay for the entertainment as he had business to attend to – but he would not say what business.'

I caught sight of Lady Jane listening to what Sarah had to say. Her eyes were wide with surprise and, dare I say it, empathy. I believe she was too shocked at this strange behaviour from Mr Cheshire to think of gloating about Sarah's love life.

'And then after dinner,' Sarah continued in a sad voice, 'when I hoped he would walk about the Glass Gallery with me, he disappeared again. I called after him and he said he was joining Robert Neale for some fishing.' For a moment I felt very relieved to hear this, but Sarah had not finished. Her green eyes flashed as she continued. 'But then I saw Robert, and he knew nothing about any "fishing". I fear my love loves me no more.'

What had Daniel Cheshire been doing that he had to lie to Lady Sarah? He may not have been fishing this afternoon, but had he been fishing earlier for a priceless catch – Her Majesty's precious crown!?

No, I could not believe he had anything to do with the theft. He is a brave and honourable man. I have seen much of his loyalty to the Queen (and to Sarah, whom he seems to love deeply). But I had needed to find someone who had been missing from the morning's entertainments and I had done so. I could not ignore this lead. What had Daniel been up to and why had he lied to Sarah? That was the most damning thing of all.

'He cannot have been the only one to miss the troupe's antics,' I said desperately, hoping another name would come up.

But everyone shook their heads. The Queen had commanded we all attend while the visitors were there, and it seemed that everyone had obeyed. I turned to Lucy Throckmorton. She rarely misses anything that happens at Court.

'Did you notice any truants?' I smiled.

'Now you mention it, Grace . . .' she said with a serious air. I felt a flutter of hope. Lucy was going to name another suspect. 'I do remember thinking how strange it was that Mr Cheshire was not there.'

My hope burst like a bubble and I felt heartsick. The music started up at this moment and I came here to my chair and my daybooke. Now I am up to date with my entry. I can do nothing yet to investigate – and, I hope, exonerate – Daniel Cheshire. Mrs Champernowne is still looking my way.

Wait! A thought has just occurred to me. The notes to the Queen were written in very poor

English and were not in Mr Cheshire's hand. I
would have recognized it. Sarah has made me read
his dreadful love poems over and over. But that
could be a ruse to throw suspicion on one of the
foreign guests.

One thing I cannot fathom: why would Mr
Cheshire want to steal the crown? He is a wealthy
young man with a good position at Court. Mr
Hatton considers him one of the best of his guards.
It is a puzzle indeed.

The exchange of crown and gold is meant to
take place in an hour and I want to be there. There
is just enough time for me to follow up this lead. If
my worst suspicions are correct and Daniel is the
thief, I can stop it before the exchange – saving Her
Majesty from the humiliation and perhaps sparing
Daniel's life as well. After all, he has saved Sarah's life
before.

At last, the Mistress of the Maids is deep in
conversation with Lady Ann Courtenay. I will hide
my daybooke, find Ellie, then go in search of Mr
Cheshire. And if Mrs Champernowne's beady eyes
catch my departure, I will feign a headache or
mayhap an earache. No, that would be too rude.
The musicians are very good. A sore throat then.

(I could truly claim to have writer's cramp but that would gain me no sympathy.)

In the Great Hall, eight of the clock

This mystery is giving me more questions than answers! So much has happened in so short a time, my head is veritably buzzing. I am back in the Great Hall, hoping that I will soon be eating my supper, for I am starving! Supper is late tonight, but of course it had to be as the Queen had an appointment in the Conduit Court. She gave her visitors no excuse – everyone was simply told that supper would be after eight. She is the Queen of England and can do as she pleases. Though I dare say there was quite a bit of indignant and unimpressed muttering in the guests' quarters this evening.

I have come to the Great Hall too early, so I am sitting at an empty trestle table, taking the opportunity to record what I have found out.

After leaving the Great Hall, I made for my bedchamber. I burst through the door and startled

Ellie, who was mending my hunting kirtle, which had suffered a mishap yesterday.

'I need you,' I panted. 'We must find Daniel Cheshire. I have reason to suspect him as the thief.'

'God's elbows!' she exclaimed. 'I'll never get this sewing done. If you want me to be at your beck and call with your snooping about, you'd best stop running in the brambles with Her Majesty's dogs and ripping everything to shreds!'

'But they enjoyed themselves so much,' I protested. 'We went right up to Duke Humphrey's tower. I couldn't help it if there were a few thorns.' I took the sewing out of her hand. 'Come, Ellie – we have no time to waste.'

Ellie suddenly looked up. 'Wait, who did you say, Grace?' I realized she had not been attending my words because she had been cross that I had interrupted her work. 'You can't mean Mr Cheshire. He's such a noble, handsome gentleman and he dotes on Lady Sarah.'

'I hope with all my heart that I am wrong,' I said. 'But stranger things have happened here at Court.'

We hurried through the halls but nobody seemed to have seen Mr Cheshire at all. The young gentlemen we spoke to grinned and winked a good deal as soon as we told them our excuse for searching him out – we said we had a note for him from Lady Sarah. At last we came across a servant who said she had spotted him making for the chapel.

We were lucky that there were visitors at Court, for it meant that the grounds were well lit with torches. We were just tiptoeing along a pathway, when I suddenly saw Daniel and pulled Ellie behind the statue of a cherub. (It was a good thing the cherub was plump enough to hide the both of us!) Daniel was behaving most oddly – creeping round the chapel door. He checked that no one was in sight and slipped inside, closing it carefully behind him. Of course, now that I write this, I realize that anyone seeing Ellie and me diving behind statues would also conclude that *we* were behaving strangely.

'Quick,' I hissed to my tiring woman. 'Follow me!'

We tiptoed to the chapel. I grasped the big metal ring on the door and turned it very, very slowly, praying that it would not clunk. We could hear muttered voices, but they did not sound too close to us. We slipped inside and crawled for the safety of a pillar. Sitting on the dusty floor, not daring to move, I could hear Ellie's quickened breathing in my ear and felt my own heart pounding. We could not risk being discovered.

I steeled myself to look round the pillar. There were two figures standing in the shadow of an archway near the altar. One of them was Daniel. The other was a man I had not seen before. They were speaking very low and, try as I might, I could not hear a word of their speech. I cast about in my mind to find innocent reasons for Daniel's behaviour but I could not help concluding that he had some bad purpose in mind. My heart bled for Lady Sarah. How would she ever recover from the knowledge that her Daniel, whom she loves dearly, was nothing but a thief and blackmailer?

Ellie suddenly gripped my arm so hard I nearly cried out. Her eyes were watering and her cheeks red. 'Going to sneeze!' she hissed.

I pointed to the door and we scuttled out into the courtyard, where we dived for another statue to hide us. (It was a minor Greek god this time.) Ellie held her nose. 'Gone now!' She grinned.

It was as well she did not sneeze – for, at that moment, Daniel came creeping out of the chapel, looking as nervous as before. He strode away through the arch that leads to the main gatehouse. We followed him into the palace, finding dark corners to leap into every time he looked round. Which he did ten times. Faith, the man was jumpy! And that gave me more cause to think he was guilty.

We must have walked, or rather crept, along passageways for miles! As soon as anyone came by, we sauntered along as if we had not a care in the world. The minute they were gone, we returned to our snooping.

'We're heading for the dairy,' whispered Ellie at last. 'What can he want here?'

'Privacy for his evil plans, no doubt!' I said. As much as I wished for it not to be true, it was becoming more and more likely that Daniel was the thief. 'The dairy is always empty at this time of day.' Mr Cheshire went into the dairy and shut the door behind him. 'There! We are thwarted again.'

'No we're not.' Ellie grinned. 'The dairy has a window to it.'

She led me through a doorway into a small courtyard and pointed. I could just see a little window high up. Ellie found a discarded barrel nearby and dragged it along so that we could both stand on it and peer in. The top looked rather rotten and the wood was green and slippery. We clung to each other and the window ledge as we strained to see into the dark room. A strong smell of curds hit our noses, which we covered with our hands. Daniel had lit a candle and was bent over a table, writing furiously. What else could he be doing so secretively but penning another demand to the Queen?

'I must get hold of that note!' I hissed. 'There is only one thing to do. I must confront him.'

Ellie was so shocked by my bold decision, she nearly fell off the barrel. When we had finally managed to climb – or rather, *slip* – down, I ran back to the herb garden and hastily gathered some lavender stalks to use as an excuse for my being in this place after dark. Then we went back into the passageway and waited outside the room.

'This is stupid, Grace!' Ellie told me in an undertone. 'Going up to a tricksy thief, bold as you like – you could be putting yourself in danger. What are you going to say? "Hello, Mr Cheshire. Give us back the Queen's crown, please." You can't do that, so come away now!' Her hand flew to her mouth. 'Too late. Here he is!'

The door to the dairy opened and Daniel came out cautiously. I started walking along, smelling my lavender, as if I had not the least idea in the world that he was there. I managed to bump into him quite heavily. He could not help but stop. (Well, I suppose I have had plenty of practice at bumping into people accidentally, so I made a good performance of it.)

'I beg your pardon, Mr Cheshire,' I said brightly. 'I did not see you in the dark passage. I was just fetching some lavender. Let me make amends by delivering that note you have in your hands. I wager it is for Lady Sarah, for she tells me you write to her every day, and often more than once.'

'No . . . I thank you . . .' muttered Daniel, turning pale and clutching the note tightly to him. 'Please excuse me . . . I am in a hurry . . .'

'It would be no trouble,' I persisted.

'No . . . No . . . it is impossible.' He looked around wildly and then began to push past. 'I beg your leave.'

With that, he was gone. I felt as if my heart were full of lead. Daniel Cheshire had always seemed such an honourable man, and so faithful to Lady Sarah, even when it was feared that her face might have been scarred for life when she was caught in a fire at St Bartholomew's Fair. Yet how could he be innocent after what we had just seen?

Ellie crept up on me. 'You were lucky there, Grace,' she said in an awed sort of voice. 'You could have been run through, or worse!'

I was not quite sure what could be worse than being run through, but there was no time to argue. We came out into the Cellar Court and I caught sight of the clock there. It was nearly seven – time for the Queen's meeting with the thief! No doubt that was why Daniel Cheshire was in such a hurry! Although I dreaded the moment, I knew I had to be there. Ellie was most relieved to scuttle back to her sewing, after many warnings that I should keep clear of flying arrows when the fiend was brought down.

I made for the gallery that looked out over the Conduit Court. It was full of armed guards, so I went up another flight of stairs to the windows over the Great Archway. From there I had a good view of the courtyard below, brightly lit by more torches than usual. I made sure to stay in the shadows.

The cart stood ready with a horse in its shafts, which stamped impatiently. Its head was being held by one of the Guard. The cart was piled high with wooden crates – supposedly with the gold in.

The chimes would be sounding any minute. My thoughts were in turmoil. For one mad moment

I wished I could warn Daniel of his fate, but squashed the idea straight away. If he was guilty, he must suffer the consequences!

The big double doors on the other side of the courtyard slowly opened. There stood Her Majesty, her silver armour gleaming in the flickering light of the torches. I gasped in awe. She looked so composed and brave. The Captain of the Guard was at her side. He too was wearing armour. Behind them stood the Jewel Master. The Queen must have told him about the ransom. Of course, she would need him to verify it truly was the crown of St Edward, for he would be the best qualified of anyone at Court to spot a forgery.

I detected slight movements at windows all around. The archers were ready to hit their target. I hoped the thief would not see them too. It might scare him away.

And now the clock struck seven. The chimes seemed to take for ever to finish resounding round the walls. Then there was silence. The Queen, Mr Hatton and Mr Bennett were as still as the stone statues that decorated the courtyard. My eyes scanned the shadows anxiously. No one appeared.

I do not know how long the Queen stood there. The silence seemed to stretch on for ever, and *still* the thief did not make his appearance. Was he watching, I wondered, revelling in the torture he was inflicting on the powerless Queen?

At last Her Majesty turned on her heel with an oath and swept back through the doors. I could tell from the toss of her head that she was beside herself with fury.

I flew down the two flights of stone stairs and ran so as to catch up with the Queen before she reached her Privy Chambers. I wanted to hear what was to be done next, though I did not dare let Her Majesty see me. I was supposed to be in the Great Hall with all the guests. I suddenly ran into a crowd of guards and could hear the Queen's angry voice in the middle of them. I stayed at a good distance where I could watch unseen.

'Never have I been so humiliated!' she was shouting to Mr Hatton and the attending guards as she was unstrapped from her armour. None dared look her in the face and Tobias Bennett bowed his head so deeply his chin was on his chest.

Although all her guests were being entertained with music and the Great Hall was some distance away, I was still a little anxious that someone might hear her ranting. The Queen has a very strident voice when she chooses.

'How dare this man toy with me!' she thundered, kicking her breastplate, which now lay on the floor. Secretary Cecil came to her side. I imagined he was going to try to calm her. 'I want him found immediately,' she growled. 'I do not care what it takes. And when I have him, he shall be squashed like a worm under my foot – but not before he has delivered my crown to me!'

'Your Majesty . . .' Mr Secretary Cecil spoke fearfully and I soon realized that what he was saying was more likely to fuel her fury than extinguish it. 'I have found another note from the thief. It was among my papers.' He held out a parchment.

I started at this. Was it the note Ellie and I had seen Daniel writing? It looked similar, though the room had been dark. I had to think through what I had just heard.

It would have been the simplest thing in the world for Daniel to put the note among Mr Secretary Cecil's papers while everyone else was either in the Great Hall or waiting for the thief to appear in the Conduit Court.

Her Majesty was glaring at the parchment with a look that could almost have set it alight! '*I take your crown to Spain soon*,' she read. 'So the villain is likely Spanish!' Her eyes flashed as she read on. '*But first I will see you tomorrow when all of Europe are mocking a Queen without a crown. And I think I will win this game of cat and mouse, for your dullard of a captain and his men are so slow they could not catch a snail.'* The Queen threw the parchment to the ground. 'Phah! If I could, I would have every member of that nation flogged and tortured until someone tells me who it is.'

With that she stormed away with Mr Hatton, the Jewel Master and assorted guards running along in her wake. Secretary Cecil quickly bent down and retrieved the note and bustled after them.

What on earth could Daniel Cheshire's connection be with Spain? I wondered. Perhaps it was more tricks to lead Hatton astray. There was but one thing I could do – track him down again and try to find out. I needed proof to lay before the Queen and Mr Hatton. Then he could be arrested, and we would have the crown back. Mayhap we should search his room. That would be a job for Masou. But for now, I would ask Ellie to come with me in my search for Daniel.

I must say that she quickly got over the relief of seeing that I was not stuck with arrows like a pin cushion.

'I'll come if I must,' she grumbled after I had

told her what had happened. 'Though it'll be next Christmas before I get your kirtle finished! At this rate you'll be running after the man more than Lady Sarah ever did. And putting yourself in the way of danger again an' all.'

'I have no choice, Ellie,' I said. 'The celebration is tomorrow. The thief, by his own admission, is still here at Placentia – therefore the crown is sure to be here too. I must find both. And Daniel Cheshire certainly has something to hide.'

'So you need me to keep you safe,' muttered Ellie. 'As usual.'

'I do not need keeping safe,' I assured her, 'but two heads are better than one.'

'Huh!' sniffed Ellie. 'Then I reckon I've got 'em both, for you seem to have lost yours.'

We tracked Daniel down to a curtained-off alcove in the Glass Gallery. I peeped between the curtain and the wall. He was sitting on the window seat, scribbling yet another note! I could not believe it. Was he writing yet another missive of mockery? He was certainly aiming to rub salt into Her Majesty's wound. Every so often he muttered an oath under his breath, crumpled up the writing and threw it to the floor, where it joined countless others. Then he would start again with a fresh parchment. I felt quite angry to see him there. It is one of my favourite places to sit and write. I had been there only hours before. I vowed I never would again after such a villain had sullied it!

'I will not approach him this time,' I whispered to Ellie as we peered round the arras.

'Heaven be praised!' put in my friend.

'I shall let *you* do it,' I went on, 'while I retrieve one of those pieces of paper on the floor. There is certain to be a clue on it.'

'Me!?' Ellie squeaked. 'He's a desperate man, Grace! He might get violent. Suppose he thinks I've come to arrest him or something?'

I smiled inwardly at the thought of Ellie arresting anyone.

'You can just be the innocent tiring woman,' I whispered. 'He will have no reason to be violent with you.'

'And what do I say to him?'

'You'll think of something,' I said, pushing her through the curtain. I watched and waited for my chance.

Daniel Cheshire leaped up when Ellie appeared before him, and nearly knocked over his ink pot. I could see that his hands were trembling as he feverishly gathered together his scattered papers.

A villain's guilt!

'Mr Cheshire,' said Ellie with a bobbing curtsy and a beaming smile. 'I would like your opinion on a very important matter. Lady Sarah' – he started at the mention of her name – 'keeps demanding my advice about what she should wear. I'm worried you might not like what I choose for her. I would hate to be—'

'Do not ask me,' he muttered distractedly. 'My opinion is worthless.'

I got down on my hands and knees and lifted the curtain an inch. There was one crumpled note still lying on the floor at his feet. I had just got my fingers round it when the curtain was flung from my hand. Daniel stormed out of the alcove. And I was sure he'd seen me!

A moment later

I have had to move to a stool in the corner, for the tables are being prepared for supper and I was in the way.

Mr Cheshire did not linger. He strode away. Ellie

and I looked at each other. A thousand fears went through my mind. If Daniel Cheshire had indeed seen me as I feared, what would he do about it? Had I put Ellie's life in danger as well as my own? What would become of Her Majesty's crown if he knew someone had discovered his plotting?

I slowly opened the note. I did not want to read what I thought I would find there. There was only one thing that gave me a crumb of comfort. Daniel had looked horror-stricken at the name of his beloved Sarah. Mayhap the fiend still had enough conscience to feel guilty about how she would suffer.

I read out loud – for Ellie cannot read herself, and I could see she was itching to know what the letter held.

'*Sarah, my dearest life*,' he writes. '*I beg you* – but that is crossed out. He begins again: *It would make me a very happy man if you* . . . That is crossed out too.'

Ellie looked perplexed and I burst out laughing.

I felt a huge flood of relief. 'Daniel is no thief,' I explained. 'And no blackmailer, either. He writes on: *I have spoken to your father, and mine, and the Queen has granted her permission. That is why I have been from your side, my dear love. Ah, how I have yearned for the courage to face you with my proposal. But it has proved more frightening than facing Her Majesty in one of her rages.* This last part is crossed out as well. I do not blame the man! *Agree to marry me*, he goes on, *and put me out of my misery.*'

Ellie grinned broadly. 'Poor man! Trying to write a proposal and we keep popping up wherever he goes!'

'And he finds me on the floor with my bum sticking up in the air!' I giggled. 'But seriously, I am so happy for Sarah. It is the one bright thing in a dark day. Ellie, we must keep this secret to ourselves.' I took her hand. 'I will release you to go to your mending at last. Thank you for helping me to clear up one mystery, but alas, I am no further forward with the other.' I felt the weight again of letting down the Queen. 'I still have no suspect – and tomorrow is coming dangerously close!'

The servants are approaching to prepare the tables for supper. At last! I think I will fall off my stool with hunger if I do not eat soon. As soon as all the Court and guests are here I shall gnaw away at this mystery like a beaver. After I have gnawed away at my supper. I will leave no stone unturned or Spaniard unquestioned. The crown must be found by tomorrow – so must the thief. If only the Queen could wear one of her other crowns at the ceremony . . . But that will not do. Everyone, except the Maids of Honour, has seen the crown of St Edward on display and will be expecting to see it on her head as promised.

But I must look on the bright side. At least now I have only one nation to investigate!

In the Great Hall during supper, near nine of the clock

I have a strong lead in the mystery! My daybooke is in my lap at the table and I am adding to it when I get the chance. And not only words – for I seem to have gathered a feast of crumbs where the pages are bound together.

The Queen has not joined us for supper. A message was sent to our guests that she had matters of State to attend to and would take a bite to eat while she did so. I believe she did not want to be faced with all the guests, not now she believes that one of them is the thief.

As we were taking our places, I first attempted to sit with some of the Spanish retinue. I planned to make innocent conversation about the festivities, hoping someone would let something slip – I might find out who had been missing this morning, apart from the lovesick Daniel. Most of the men just ignored me, but one nobleman – a man with a huge curled moustache – rudely turned his back! The ladies did converse with me, but they acted very superior and made many veiled comments about the English and their lack of fashion. If I was looking for a suspect who did not like England, then I had found plenty!

I gave up, for my stomach was growling loudly now, and went and sat with Mrs Champernowne and Mary Shelton. The Mistress of the Maids leaned over the table and patted my arm.

'It does you credit, Lady Grace,' she said, 'that you try to make our visitors welcome. There was no call for them to behave so badly.' She must have seen the whole of it. 'And I would advise you not to go near that Don Fernando de la Garza again.' She gave a disapproving sniff towards the man with the big moustache who had turned his back on me. 'Though we knew him as Fernando Hathaway, look you.'

Mary and I both looked at her in surprise.

'You know him, Mrs Champernowne?' asked Mary.

'His father, John, was one of King Henry's Court,' she told us, settling down to enjoy telling her tale. 'John Hathaway married a Spanish woman and they lived a good life until he started speaking out against the King and his foreign policy. They say his wife was influencing him, turning him towards Spain. King Henry did not like it, so he removed him from Court and took his lands, leaving him penniless. John Hathaway died of the shame of it, or so it was believed. Anyhow, his widow and her four children had to go back to Spain.'

I gasped. 'That's terrible.'

I glanced over at the moustachioed noble. I had not looked properly at him before – he had turned his back on me too quickly! But now I had leisure to take in his features.

'You know,' I said musingly, 'I must have seen him before. He reminds me of someone, but I cannot think who.'

'It is unlikely,' said Mrs Champernowne. 'This is the first time he has returned to England since he was eight years old. I am surprised to see him now. He has shown nothing but contempt for his English

roots. Calling himself only by his mother's name –
de la Garza – and being as thoroughly unpleasant as
he can to everyone here!'

I actually thought he had good reason, though I
dared not say so to Mrs Champernowne. She had
told a dreadful story that would have been rather
depressing had I not been tingling with excitement
– for here was a very likely suspect. Señor de la
Garza – or Señor Moustache, as he had become
fixed in my mind – had no love for the English, and
might well have stolen the crown to humiliate the
Queen. And the ransom note had said that the thief
would be taking the crown to Spain.

There was one way to find out if he was a likely
suspect.

'I expect he turned his nose up at the troupe's
display this morning,' I said. 'Did you see him
there?'

Mrs Champernowne thought long and hard.
'Now, I was standing near the Spanish Ambassador
and his people . . . Doña Francesca was there
because I admired her pearls, and Señor Gomez . . .'
She went through a long list of Spaniards who
had been there. I tried not to fidget but she
was taking an age. 'You know, Grace,' she
announced at last, 'I do believe Señor de la Garza

was absent. What an insult to Her Majesty!'

This was sounding better and better – for a moment.

'He was there, Mrs Champernowne,' said Mary. 'Do you not remember? He sat near Lord Robert Dudley. He had a sour face throughout, which made Lord Robert angry.'

No! I wanted to cry out. Was I to find a good suspect only to have him taken away in an instant? I was so frustrated, I was actually somewhat angry at Mary for being the one to burst my most recent bubble, which was unfair – it was not *her* fault de la Garza might be innocent.

'Are you sure?' I asked. 'With their hats and ruffs, many of the Spanish gentlemen look alike.'

Poor Mary seemed quite confused for a moment and I felt my hopes rise again.

'Yes, I am certain,' she said decidedly. 'Who could forget that moustache? And he said something very unkind about Masou "apeing his betters".'

I longed for this man to be the villain, for he had insulted my dear friend Masou. But de la Garza had been in full view at the time of the robbery, so he could not have stolen the crown. I was back to the beginning again.

★   ★   ★

I have faithfully recorded that important information without getting many more crumbs in my daybooke. Now I must lay it aside and look interested in the conversation around me. Mrs Champernowne is making disapproving faces as I write. God's Oath! I must needs find a new suspect, and quickly, for tomorrow fast approaches. How long will I have to sit here before I can get on with it?

A little later, still in the Great Hall

Supper is now over. As soon as it had been cleared the Queen swept into the Great Hall and demanded dancing! She looked wonderful in her gown of black velvet. The sleeves and partlet were encrusted with pearls and fine netting, and she wore a magnificent ruby brooch. We all bowed and curtsied before her and I felt my heart swell with admiration. No one could possibly guess what fury must be raging inside her. She glanced about the hall with a bright glint in her eyes that brooked no defeat. It has given me strength. I am more determined than ever to find the thief.

But first I am obliged to dance. I am sitting with Mary Shelton and, even now, she is pestering me to lay aside my quill. I do not like to dance – but that is the lot of a Maid of Honour, so I must. This is so frustrating. I want to be investigating, not hopping about pretending to enjoy a Galliard.

About twenty minutes later

Something most mysterious has just happened. I am keeping a sweet smile on my face to try and show that there is nothing amiss. Inside I am boiling with rage . . . and a little fear. My identity as Her Majesty's Lady Pursuivant might be known!

When I went to dance, I put my quill inside my penner and placed it with my daybooke under Mrs Champernowne's chair. She was talking to Lady Margaret Mortimer and did not notice.

Mary dragged me onto the floor and a Galliard began. I looked about, hoping I could deflect the 'obligation' onto another of my fellow Maids. But they were all otherwise engaged in the dancing – all except Lucy Throckmorton, who I could not see anywhere. I assumed she was off eavesdropping or gossiping. Thus I was left with no choice but to dance my feet off! Of course, I did not really – but it felt like it. First my hand was claimed by Mr Bennett, who was charming – although I could see the anxiety about the theft was not far from his eyes. Then there was a Dutch merchant, then a diplomat from Saxony, and finally a brave Mr Westerland. I say brave because I have not always been a good partner if you love your toes! However, my dancing has improved greatly since my secret lesson back in September, and I could see Mr Westerland was impressed – and probably very relieved. And I will just remark here – as I am proud of the fact – that, for once, not one of my partners limped back to his seat afterwards!

I hoped that my duty was done and I could return to my chair when, to my surprise, Señor Moustache held out his hand for the Pavane. His face was as unsmiling as ever but I could not refuse. It was a very strange affair. He said not a word to me but stared above my head. It sounds fanciful, but I got a cold feeling from him. He does remind me of someone, but I cannot think who.

The music ended and I fled back to my chair before another man could ask me to dance. I had decided to write about Señor Moustache and so had gathered up my penner. But when I reached for my daybooke, I thought my heart would stop with the shock. It had gone!

I scrabbled about under the chair searching for it. It *had* to be there. I could not bear the thought of anyone else reading it. There were too many secrets written down. And my identity as Lady Pursuivant would be known. My success at solving mysteries is partly due to no one knowing what I am about, and seeing only a Maid of Honour. But much worse would be the disgrace brought upon me, for the Queen could never show public approval of one of her Maids undertaking such missions.

I had to find my book. There was no sign of it where I was sitting, so I began to walk about the company. My ferreting was sure to raise suspicion, so I pretended I was looking for Mary. (She was actually out of the hall at that moment, for the lace on her hem had torn and she had been whisked away by her tiring woman, Fran. But I did not let on I knew that.)

I felt my hand grasped. It was Robert Neale, a plump young courtier.

'Would you do me the honour?' he asked with a bow.

I could not refuse but, in truth, I did not pay the music or the dance much attention. I was too busy thinking and made the steps automatically. Who could have taken my daybooke?

Mr Neale suddenly lifted me up in the air. I had no idea we were dancing a Volta until then and let out a shriek of surprise! Poor Robert was quick to shed me when the music ended and I was free to get back to my thoughts.

Who would want to steal my daybooke? Well, it could only be someone who thought there was something within the pages that was of interest to them; which meant that someone at Court had observed me always writing, and had thought it rather strange. Only a guilty heart would connect such an act . . .

The crown thief!

If it was the crown thief who had stolen my daybooke, then he would know that I was investigating him. A cold feeling of dread crept over me. I might be in grave danger. Well, that could not be helped. Danger had not stopped me before. But now he would be as much on his guard in my presence as he would with Mr Hatton and my advantage would be lost. And surely he would not risk staying at Court any longer. He would flee immediately, taking the crown with him. It would be lost for ever!

I pushed my way through the throng, trying to get back to my seat. I had a dreadful compulsion to cry but managed not to.

'Excuse me. I beg your pardon!' I murmured in a daze as I trod on a toe here and elbowed someone else there. My daybooke, with all its secrets, was in someone else's hands, I was no closer to catching the thief, and tomorrow was the grand ceremony where the Queen was going to wear her coronation crown but there was no crown for her to wear. What was I going to do?

I bumped into Sarah, who was standing on her own. She looked very pale and woebegone. If only I could tell her that Daniel was going to ask her to marry him very soon. But I could not. Another secret to be kept.

'Do not fret about Daniel,' I said to her as I passed. 'I am sure he will be back at your side as soon as he can.'

Sarah merely sniffed and tossed her head.

At last I found myself with Mrs Champernowne again. I felt for my penner under her chair, meaning to make some excuse and leave. My fingers closed around . . . my daybooke! I was so pleased to have it back that I could have danced all round the Great Hall on my own. But the question remained. Who had taken it? I believe they had put it back hoping that I would never realize it had been missing. I would have to hold my tongue and ask no questions.

And in case the daybooke thief was watching, I opened it up and began this entry. I am behaving like Her Majesty. If she can overcome her inner feelings and maintain an outer calm, then so can I. I wonder if her face aches like mine does. The sweet smile is hard to maintain. I have my precious daybooke back but I want to know who dared to take it in the first place! I was busy dancing when it was taken.

However, I must put that aside for the moment. The return of the crown is my most pressing concern, and time is running out. I must get my thoughts in order.

What do I know about the crown thief?

He can write, so he is an educated man.

He has a clever mind.

The theft had taken some planning.

It was very fast planning, for no one knew the jewels would be here before this morning.

He also worked out that the panel in the

storeroom ceiling could be removed.

He cleverly thought of using the fishing line so that he did not have to enter the room at all.

He is a bitter person who wants to see the Queen suffer.

He is still at Court because he will want to see with his own eyes Her Majesty's humiliation when she appears at the ceremony tomorrow to celebrate her coronation, without her coronation crown. Though, of course, that is not going to happen. I will not permit it!

But what evidence do I have? None!

And yet I keep seeing Señor Moustache in my head. He hates the English and he gives me that cold feeling. He may not have done the actual theft – for he was seen at the morning's entertainment – but I have a suspicion he may still be involved somehow. Call it instinct, but the Queen did tell me to use my instinct.

There was certainly something odd about his wanting to dance with me. I wonder if he was distracting me for some reason . . . Yes! To keep me away so that his accomplice could purloin my precious daybooke. But who was this accomplice?

Fie! Just when I thought I was getting closer to the answer, more questions stand in my way like Gentlemen Guard.

I have to get away and think about this some more. I should tell Mrs Champernowne that I am just returning my daybooke and penner to my bedchamber – and, of course, should beg leave to depart from the Queen. But that will take an age and she may say no! So I will try to slip out through a door. There are guards on each entrance, but the one nearest to the kitchen has a great hustle and bustle about it as refreshments are brought in. Perhaps I shall dodge a servant with a loaded tray, and if that happens to take me through the doorway, then so be it!

I will go straight to my room, because I want to hide my daybooke away securely. Then I will find Ellie and search the chambers of the Spanish while they are busy dancing. I know Mr Hatton's men have already done that, but they are sometimes hasty and may have missed something.

I have just remembered I still have the stalks of lavender I picked earlier. I will take them with me and if anyone catches us prying in the Spanish bedchambers, I will say that we are merely carrying out an old English custom, laying a sprig of lavender on a guest's pillow. (If it isn't already an old English custom, it should be.)

The Fifteenth Day of January, in the Year of Our Lord 1571

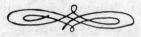

Early – in my bedchamber

Sarah and Mary are asleep, but I am up with the lark! I have slept – in the Queen's bed – but have now risen and come back here to get my daybooke. I have only a small stub of candle and much to write so I hope the first will outlast the second.

Last night, when I escaped from the Great Hall, I found Ellie in my bedchamber laying out my nightdress.

'Come,' I said, fishing two cloaks out of my clothes press. 'We are going spying!'

I held out the cloak she had chosen from the Queen's chests. 'Wear this, for it is a cold night.'

Her eyes lit up as she wrapped the black velvet round her. 'To think I'm wearing a cape of Her Majesty's!' she said. Then she frowned. 'What do you mean, "we are going spying"?'

I told her that I wanted to search the Spanish lodgings.

'Sounds dangerous to me,' she said. 'But I'm not going to pass up a chance to wear this cloak.'

I grabbed the lavender and we left, walking swiftly along the passages.

'Are you sure about going to their lodgings?' asked Ellie. 'I know time is running out, but isn't it a bit foolish, Grace? They're from overseas, after all. Who knows what sort of things we'll find in their rooms. Remember the Bandy Yasmin, or whatever you called her? She had a panther in her bedchamber!'

'Rajah was lovely.' I smiled at her. 'We will be careful. And what choice do we have? You said it yourself. Time is running out.'

We crossed the Conduit Court (for what felt like the hundredth time today) towards the chambers assigned to the Spanish guests. We were just about to go inside when we heard low voices. I pulled Ellie behind a statue of a centaur. (These statues have never proved more useful!)

Two men came into view. The first was Tobias Bennett. Then, in the gloomy torchlight, I recognized the man behind him. It was Señor de la Garza. The Jewel Master must have the same suspicions as I and was questioning him. Mayhap he had some actual evidence. This could bode well for the return of the crown!

The two men passed our hiding place and made for the Spanish quarters.

I nudged Ellie and we followed them, keeping to the shadows. They were talking in quiet voices, but we caught some of their conversation.

'Is it all arranged?' Señor Moustache spoke in English with barely a trace of an accent. That was not surprising, of course. He had lived in England until he was eight. What *was* surprising was that it did not sound as if Mr Bennett was doing the questioning. I leaned forward to hear more.

'I have made sure that the horses are very fast,' Mr Bennett was saying.

'And we leave tonight?'

'After the dancing,' the Jewel Master told him. 'We cannot go before. We would be missed.'

God's Oath! I had found Señor Moustache's accomplice – none other than the Queen's loyal servant, Tobias Bennett! I felt Ellie stiffen beside me.

'Then we must get back to the Great Hall without delay,' I heard Mr Bennett say. '*A medianoche – la fragua.*'

I rubbed my ears hard. Was I hearing things? Surely he had just spoken in Spanish – and fluently too, with a good accent.

Ellie pinched my arm. 'He spoke foreign,' she hissed.

My ears had not deceived me.

The two men clasped hands.

'*Mi hermano!*' declared Señor Moustache as they went back towards the Great Hall.

'What did they say?'

'I do not know,' I whispered back. 'It was Spanish. But I think *medianoche* is midnight. So they must be planning to meet somewhere at twelve this evening. I'll warrant *la fragua* is the place they are meeting, but *mi hermano* could be anything.'

Despite the cold I sat back on my heels. I felt as if I had been punched in the stomach. Everything seemed turned on its head. How could this be?

Mr Bennett had been in loyal service at the Tower for years. He came from a well-respected family who had passed down the position of Jewel Master – hence his pure grief when the theft occurred.

He could not be involved with the theft, could

he? But, if he was innocent of any wrong doing, why was he conspiring with Señor Moustache? To my mind, there could be only one answer.

'I think the Jewel Master could not be involved. Only the finest man could be elevated to his position. It must be an elaborate ploy,' I said to Ellie. 'I think Mr Bennett is pretending to be an accomplice in order to get the crown back. Señor Moustache thinks that they will escape together when, really, Mr Bennett will alert Mr Hatton's men and have him arrested there.'

'Why can't he be arrested now?' demanded Ellie.

'Perhaps Mr Bennett does not know where the crown is, and is waiting for it to be revealed. Perhaps we can act as a back-up. If we are at the meeting, we might be able to help, in case anything goes wrong. Find Masou. He knows some Spanish. See if he can tell you what *la fragua* is. Then ask him to meet us there well before midnight. I must get back to the Queen before I am missed.'

Taking my cloak, Ellie scurried off towards the troupe's quarters and I returned to the Great Hall. I was just in time! The Queen was taking her leave early and everyone was bowing and curtsying. The excuse was that she needed to be well-rested for the ceremony tomorrow. I did not think she would get much rest. She would be frantic with worry about her crown.

I was lucky that everyone had their eyes on the floor, which meant I was able to creep in and crouch into a curtsy, albeit rather clumsily, as if I had been there all along. When the Queen had gone, I stood up and found myself next to Mary Shelton. She raised her eyebrows at me but said nothing. What good fortune that it was Mary! I can always rely on her to keep her own counsel. Lady Jane or Carmina – or Lucy Throckmorton – would have decided that I had been off with an admirer and I would never have heard the end of it.

Back in our bedchamber, Ellie was putting away my earrings, but I could not ask her if she had spoken to Masou in front of my fellow Maids.

'Why are you not in your nightgown, Grace?' asked Sarah as Olwen brushed her hair.

'I will be soon enough,' I said quickly. 'I have to . . .' Fie! I had done so much quick thinking during my investigation that I had run out of lies – my mind went as blank as the first page of a daybooke.

'She has to be taken off for one more fitting, my lady,' cut in Ellie, saving me for a second time that day. 'Lady Grace does not stand as still as you and' – she dropped her voice – 'the tailors have had a devil of a job with her.'

Clever Ellie. Sarah asked no more. In truth I was worried about Sarah. She looked so pale and sad. I wondered if she believed she had lost her faithful suitor. If only I could tell her the truth – but surely Daniel would speak soon.

I had to wait for Mary Shelton and Lady Sarah to fall asleep before I could sneak out. Luckily, they were both soon snoring. But I had heard the chimes sound half past eleven some minutes ago, so Ellie and I had to make haste.

We slipped along the passage.

'Masou said *la fragua* means the forge,' she told me.

'Then that is where we will meet him,' I whispered. 'I wish there had been time to make a Grace shape in the bed.'

'I thought of that.' Ellie grinned. 'If we are discovered, you can just yawn and blink and say "Oh, am I sleepwalking?"'

'And what would be your excuse?' I demanded.

'I thought of that too.' Ellie sounded smug. 'I would say I'd followed you to make sure you came to no harm, but I knew I mustn't ever wake a sleepwalker.'

'You think of everything, Ellie,' I said
admiringly. She may not be able to read or write,
but her wits are much sharper than many highborn
courtiers I can think of.

We hurried across the palace grounds to the
forge. It was at the end of a row of workshops by
the armoury. The way was well-lit with torches. A
shape suddenly slipped out from behind a nearby
bush. We started and clutched each other in fear.

'Greetings, o fair ones.' It was Masou, and he
looked very pleased with himself.

'That didn't work,' scolded Ellie. 'You never
scared us!'

In the torchlight I could see Masou's look of
injured innocence. 'Scare you, dear Ellie?' he
exclaimed, wide-eyed. 'On the contrary, I am here
as your protector.'

'There's no time to waste with silliness,' I told
him. 'We must be at the forge before twelve.'

But as we drew near, we could see lights
flickering through the window and hear sounds of
laughter.

'They are already here,' whispered Masou.

'Mr Hatton's men have not arrived yet,' I said.
'But Mr Bennett must surely have alerted them.'

We crept up to the window of the forge, and

carefully peered in through the dirty glass. What a sight lay before us! The embers of the fire were still glowing from the day's work and a candle flickered on the anvil. Mr Bennett sat on the floor with Señor Moustache. They had tankards in front of them. As we watched, they clanged the tankards together with a splash and drank deeply. It seemed that the Jewel Master was keeping Señor Moustache busy so that he did not think of escaping before the Guard had time to arrive.

Then Mr Bennett looked about him. He rapped out something in Spanish.

'What is he saying?' I hissed.

Masou cupped his ear. 'Mr Bennett has bribed one of the servants and says that the horses will be here soon,' he whispered. 'Truly, the Jewel Master is a fine actor to have fooled this criminal.'

The two men now clasped each other round the shoulders and burst into song. I could only make out a few words – and there was one that Señor Moustache had used before.

'What does *mi hermano* mean?' I asked Masou as they sang. I had forgotten all about it until now. 'Señor Moustache said it to Mr Bennett earlier.'

'Easy.' Masou grinned. 'It means "my brother".'

The truth stabbed through me like a knife.

Suddenly I knew why Señor Moustache had looked familiar to me earlier. Take away those elaborate whiskers and he looked like an older Mr Bennett. The Jewel Master was his younger brother! He must be a Hathaway, I reasoned, his early years spent in Spain after his family's disgrace. That was why he spoke the language so well. He was not here to trick Señor Moustache and recover the crown at all. They were in this dastardly plot together!

But how had he wormed his way into his position at the Tower? Only the most trusted worked in the Jewel House.

One thing was certain. He had stolen the crown and was planning to flee the country tonight. It was he who sought the Queen's humiliation at the celebrations tomorrow. I told my friends what I had deduced.

'I never thought to ask if Mr Bennett had been present at the entertainments,' I said. 'How stupid of me! He must have seen off the last visitors and locked the door in the sight of the guards. But he had already secretly drugged his men. When he knew they would be deeply asleep, he climbed up onto the roof to fish for the crown.'

'The clapper-clawed bugbear!' hissed Ellie. She

clenched her fists. 'There's three of us and only two of them. Let's get 'em!'

'A brave thought, Ellie,' whispered Masou. 'They may be two, but they are grown men. We could not match them in strength.'

'Nor do we know where the crown is,' I said, 'and that must be our first concern. What a victory it would be for England, for the celebrations to go ahead tomorrow, with the Queen wearing her symbol of royalty as planned!'

My eyes flew round every shadow in the room, searching for signs of the crown. I wished I could clean the window, but that would certainly be noticed by the blackguards!

Then Mr Bennett – I still called him that, though his name must be Hathaway, I supposed – lifted up a candle. He was telling his brother something in an excited voice.

'What's he saying?' demanded Ellie.

'It is too fast,' said Masou apologetically.

As the Jewel Master waved the candle about, something glinted sharply in the corner of the room. I blinked and looked again. It would have to be a shiny object to have flashed so in the light. And then I saw it, half concealed by a bit of sacking – the crown! What I saw next made me feel sick to my stomach. Mr Bennett picked it up, lifted it high in the air – and placed it on his head! Ellie gasped and Masou muttered a curse under his breath at the sight.

'The evil-eyed hedge-pig!' Ellie grabbed my sleeve as the nefarious Jewel Master strutted about the forge and then turned to his brother.

'Look at me!' he gloated, in a silly high-pitched voice. He was speaking in English now. 'I am the Queen of England. I am a silly old woman.'

Ellie bristled beside me. 'How dare he?!' she said through gritted teeth. 'That's treason if ever I heard it!' And before we could stop her, she banged on the window!

Instantly, the door flew open. Masou and I ducked behind a crate but Ellie was not as quick. The Jewel Master – still wearing the crown – spotted her and grabbed her by the arm.

I watched him haul her roughly into the forge, my heart sinking. My dear friend was in the worst peril!

'Take that off your head!' I heard her demand. Masou and I chanced a look through the window and saw that for a second the two men were dumbfounded.

'What are you doing here?' Señor Moustache

demanded, shoving her into a corner.

Masou and I looked at each other in horror.

I thought that Ellie had immediately regretted her rash action, for she now slumped to the ground. Then, at her next words, I realized she was play-acting. 'I never meant any harm, sirs,' she whimpered. 'I was just on me way back to the palace. I sneaked out to see my sweetheart. He's a butcher's lad in the village. And I saw your light and thought you were mocking Her Majesty and stepped in . . .'

Mr Bennett took the crown off his head and began to wrap it in the sacking. 'What shall we do with her?' he growled. 'We cannot afford to have her missed and a search set up.'

Señor Moustache gave Ellie a fierce shaking. 'She is only a servant,' he shouted angrily. 'Surely no one will care about her.'

The horrible man was certainly wrong about that, and I was determined to save poor Ellie.

'I have seen this girl in the palace.' Mr Bennett's tone was firm. 'She is not *only* a servant, she is the tiring woman of one of the Maids of Honour. Believe me, she will be missed. She will have to come with us.'

'I'm not going nowhere!' Ellie shrieked.

I went cold. It was all I could do not to leap in after her.

The Jewel Master bent down and looked her in the eye. 'Oh yes, you are,' he snarled. 'We cannot afford to have you raising the alarm. So you will make a little journey to the coast, and then across the sea with us. And if you are a good girl, we will let you go when we reach France.'

Ellie gulped. 'But I don't know no French, sir.'

'Then you will have to learn.' The Jewel Master thrust a rope at his brother. 'Tie her up, Fernando, and gag her mouth. She looks like a shrieker.'

'Where's that cursed servant with the horses?' muttered Señor Moustache as he bound Ellie's hands and put a kerchief round her mouth. 'We must get away now!'

I had to make a dreadful decision. There was only one thing to do if I was to rescue my friend – and the crown of St Edward. One of us had to go for help and that had to be me. I could get access to the Queen much more easily than Masou, despite his superior speed. But I did not want to leave my poor brave Ellie alone with these knaves.

'You stay here and try to prevent them from going,' I hissed to Masou. 'I will go for help.'

He nodded gravely. 'It is the best plan.' He

rubbed his nose thoughtfully. 'Off you go, Grace. I will think of a way to slow them down.'

I picked up my skirts and ran like a hobbledehoy. There were several guards in the passage leading to the Queen's chambers. I could see the amazement on their faces as I sped towards them. For a moment I considered alerting only the guards and not Her Majesty at all – but I could not take the risk that the guards would believe me.

I knew the Queen would.

'Let me through!' I yelled.

'What are you doing here, Lady Grace?' said Henry Westerland. 'What is amiss?'

'Urgent message for Her Majesty,' I puffed, holding my side, which was developing a fierce stitch. 'Must see my godmother.'

I do not know if it was my relationship with the Queen, or because they all knew me, but the men stepped aside and let me into the Privy Chambers. Mr Westerland signalled to the guards at the next door, which led into the Privy Bedchamber. They let me pass.

Only one candle burned in the chamber. The Queen was asleep in the bed and several other Ladies-in-Waiting slept also. Lady Ann Courtenay and Lady Margaret Mortimer sat on either side of the bed, keeping watch over the Queen. They did this when she found it hard to sleep. And now I had to wake her up. I should have persuaded the guards to do it instead. I was still panting loudly from my run – and not from fear at all. The Queen was going to think there was a monster coming to get her! But the news I had could not wait.

'Lady Grace,' whispered Lady Ann. 'What are you doing here?'

'The Queen,' I croaked. 'Must wake her. Urgent message.'

Lady Margaret's eyes took on a pleading look. 'But she has only just got to sleep,' she murmured. 'Please do not disturb her.'

'Must speak . . . with my godmother,' I managed to gasp.

They shook their heads, whether in warning or sorrow I am not sure.

I took a deep breath and touched the Queen's arm.

'Your Majesty,' I said softly.

The Queen slept on.

'My Liege,' I said a bit louder. I felt a shiver of pure terror go down my spine – but I had to do this. I shook her arm.

Nothing, not even a snore!

This was getting me nowhere, and at any moment Ellie and the crown could be on the road for France.

'Elizabeth!' I yelled in her ear.

The Queen opened her eyes and sat bolt upright.

'HOW DARE YOU!' she roared, and I felt as if she would blast me all the way up Greenwich Hill. She glared about the room and the other Ladies, all awake now, cringed into the shadows. Then she focused on me and brushed her flowing hair out of her eyes. 'Lady Grace' – her tone was biting – 'explain yourself.'

I could not tell her everything in front of these witnesses so I bent forward and whispered, 'I have found the crown, Your Majesty. But we must make haste and bring guards.'

I knew I would not need to tell her more to get her to act. She has the quickest of brains, even when she has just risen from slumber. She was out of bed in a flash, calling for her robe.

'Lady Frances,' she said firmly. 'Send for Mr Hatton immediately and have him bring twenty of his finest men. And the rest of you, wait outside.'

The minute the room was empty, she demanded I tell her all. I had just got to the part where Ellie had been taken captive by Mr Bennett and his brother when Mr Hatton arrived.

'I have had a message,' she told him. 'My crown and its wretched thieves are at the forge and, if we make haste, we shall catch them there. Send your fastest men ahead, for they are even now getting ready to flee Placentia. I shall follow.'

So must I, I thought to myself. But how would I contrive it? I need not have worried.

Mr Hatton moved to the door to give the order. 'And tell them to take care,' she called after him. 'They have taken a captive. A tiring woman apparently.' She turned to me and took my hands. 'I am sorry to break this to you, Lady Grace, but it is Ellie, your servant.'

'Then I must come as well,' I declared, pretending that this was news to me.

'Of course you must,' she agreed.

The Queen is truly the most wonderful person in the whole wide world to have so quickly found a way to allow me to accompany her. Her mind would never go as blank as mine had in my bedchamber, of that I am sure.

We hurried through the palace grounds to the forge, surrounded by a retinue of guards. I prayed that Masou had been able to delay the villains and

that Mr Hatton's advance party would be in time to rescue Ellie. I did not want to think about her bundled upon a horse, galloping fast for the coast. If the Jewel Master was desperate, would he forget his words not to harm her? I could not bear the thought of anything happening to my dear friend.

My head was buzzing by the time we reached the forge. I dreaded finding the two Spaniards long gone, and Ellie with them. I might never see her again!

To my relief I could see that the villains had not gone anywhere. The door had been jammed shut by someone sticking a broom handle through the sconces on either side of it! We could hear hammering and shouting from inside. This must be Masou's handiwork, but my friend had cleverly stayed out of sight. I heard a faint hooting. It was much too close to be an owl, so I knew that Masou was telling me he was still nearby. Mr Hatton's advance guard stood waiting for their captain.

I hoped Ellie was safe. The brothers sounded furious.

A guard removed the broom and Mr Hatton flung the door open. The Jewel Master and his brother were confronted by the Captain of the

Guard and the Queen, both stern and unsmiling.
Señor Moustache was holding Ellie by the arms.

'It is finished, Mr Bennett,' said the Queen, in a
voice that would have turned the whole of the
Thames to ice. 'Hand over the girl and my crown.'

Señor Moustache seemed to become crazed.
'Spawn of the wicked King Henry' – he almost
spat the words at the Queen, shaking Ellie in his
wrath – 'you do not deserve your crown! You and
your country will sink into the sea and you will
feel the force of—YOW!'

With a yelp of pain he suddenly let go of Ellie
and leaped about the room rubbing his arm.
Ellie took advantage of her freedom and ran for
Mr Hatton. Then she turned and faced her captor.
'And you felt the force of me pin!' she yelled,
brandishing a sharp implement that she must have
kept handy about her person. (And to think she
had complained about sewing up my kirtle!)

The guards moved in and soon had Mr Bennett
and his brother held fast. I picked up the sacking
and handed the crown to the Queen. It was very
heavy. She turned it over in her hands. I could
barely breathe at the sight of it – it was truly
beautiful, its jewels glinting in the torchlight.

'Why, Mr Bennett?' she said simply. 'You had a

good position here. A good life. Why have you thrown it all away?'

'For vengeance!' the Jewel Master said angrily. 'My name is not Bennett. It is Hathaway . . . Juan Hathaway. Your cursed father ruined my family and caused the death of my father and sisters. For that, you should suffer. You should have been made to squirm in front of all your visitors. I would have enjoyed every single moment – even more than the look on your face when you realized the jewel thief was not going to appear in the courtyard at seven o'clock!'

He looked wildly around at us all. 'You are doomed,' he ranted. 'All of you. I may have failed in my task, but the war continues. England is nothing against the might of Spain and the true religion. I will have my revenge when you are all nothing but peasants.'

Mr Hatton had the de la Garza brothers taken quickly away.

'Ellie Bunting,' said the Queen, 'you have been very brave. And I have it in mind to give a reward for the recovery of my crown. There will be a purse of coins for you and' – she glanced around – 'any that helped you.'

I am convinced that she had guessed that Masou

was not far away and was including him in her thanks. I tingled with pleasure at her generosity.

Ellie fell to her knees. 'I'd do it again in a heartbeat, and not for gold, Your Majesty,' she said. Then she took a deep breath and, keeping her eyes fixed on the ground, spoke again. 'In fact, if I might make so bold . . . may I . . . instead of money . . . watch the celebrations tomorrow? I mean, today.' She gulped and looked at me in terror. Had she gone too far?

The Queen turned to Mr Hatton. 'Mr Bennett and his brother had it wrong,' she told him. I could hear the emotion in her voice. 'England will never fall, not while there are people like Ellie Bunting in this land. Yes, my loyal little tiring woman. You shall watch the celebrations *and* have a purse of coins, to boot. You have earned it.' She turned towards the palace. 'And now to bed! Come, Grace, you will sleep in my chamber. We cannot have you disturbing your fellow Maids by returning at this hour.'

When we were again in the Privy Bedchamber, the Queen sent everyone else away. Then she took my hands.

'Thank you, dear Grace,' she said, bending forward to kiss my cheek. 'You have saved the day.

The celebrations will go on in a few hours, and I will wear my crown on my head for all to see.'

She frowned as she sat on the bed. 'Although I believe the brothers were working alone in their quest for revenge, I'll warrant the Spanish authorities had wind of it and did nothing to prevent it. I am suspicious of them and what they intend for our fair island. But, for reasons of diplomacy, I must keep my counsel, and hope that Spanish hostilities to England recede.'

She lay back against the pillows. 'Now blow the candles out and get you to sleep, god-daughter. You will need your rest. I am sure to be using your skills again in the future. I must have my Lady Pursuivant in the best of health!'

I had succeeded in my task, and completed the mission Her Majesty had set for me.

And because everything was solved, I did sleep deeply.

At last I have it all in my daybooke. I have beaten the candle! I will just creep into my bed, and Sarah and Mary will have no idea what I have been up to during the night.

The Queen's Privy Chambers, just before one of the clock

I am sitting by a roaring fire in the Queen's Privy Chamber. She insisted that I sit here after the celebrations.

'You have earned yourself some peace and quiet after all your endeavours on my behalf,' she told me.

Then she harried everyone else out. She sits across from me by the fire, reading a book. But every now and then I know her eyes are upon me. I have a warm feeling inside, and it is not just from the flames.

Enough. I must write of the celebrations!

We rose early and breakfasted in our rooms. I thought I would have trouble waking after only a few hours' sleep but I think excitement had worked some magic on me for I was not aware of any tiredness.

Ellie helped me into my gown of black satin. She had been right. It was a beautiful creation with the embroidered clouds and skylarks. The tailors had been hard at work and it fitted perfectly. If it is not treason to say it, I felt like a queen.

I walked with the other Maids and Ladies-in-Waiting to the Presence Chamber. Here, the Queen joined us, looking magnificent with her hair flowing loose. She held the sceptre and orb in each hand. Across her neck was the fine ruby and diamond collar. Someone had been back to the Tower for them. I would warrant it was Mr Hatton himself.

'The very dress she wore on this day twelve years ago,' Mary Shelton whispered to me. 'And her hair is in the same fashion.'

Lord Robert Dudley and Secretary Cecil came up and took their places behind the Queen.

'Lord Robert arranged the coronation all those years ago,' Lucy was quick to add. 'And I believe this celebration was his idea.'

Behind us stood other members of the Queen's Court and now, with Her Majesty leading us, we processed in a stately fashion to the Great Hall, where the foreign visitors waited. The harbingers practically deafened us with their joyous fanfare as we entered. (I hope they deafened the Spanish! And gave Juliana, the sour-faced Hollander, earache.) While the Queen made her way to the centre of the chamber and the Court and visitors bowed, I had a quick look around. I was delighted to see a wide-eyed Ellie up in the musicians' gallery. The Queen had kept her promise, of course, and had ensured that my tiring woman had one of the best views of all. Masou was with the rest of the troupe.

The Queen stood by her Chair of State and we all sank into deep bows again. She took her place in her chair and a page stepped up bearing the crown of St Edward on a cushion. Archbishop Matthew Parker held it up above the Queen's head for a few moments and then carefully put it in its rightful place. A gasp of pleasure ran around the assembled viewers and we all cheered. The Queen did not wince once at the weight!

I thought I would burst the seams of my new dress in my pride at the scene. I was so happy that we had found the crown in time. We had saved the Queen from dreadful shame, and she seemed to glow more brightly than ever as she stepped among us, showing England in her true glory.

Refreshments were now served and we were free to talk and walk about the hall. I saw the Queen in conversation with a duke from Saxony but she beckoned me over.

'You will excuse me a moment, my lord,' she said with a sweet smile. 'I wish to remove the crown now and will need this Maid to help me with my hair.'

She led the way to her Privy Chambers and, once inside, took my hand.

'Did you enjoy the spectacle, Grace?' she asked.

'Oh yes, Your Majesty,' I said. 'With all my heart. I could imagine I was at your actual coronation.'

'It is thanks to you that the celebrations were a success,' the Queen said. 'Now, we cannot be long away from the festivities, but I wished to apprise you of what has gone on this morning.' She led me to a chair. 'Secretary Cecil had words with the Spanish Ambassador and told him of the perfidy of Mr Bennett and Señor de la Garza.'

'Was the Ambassador shocked?' I asked.

'Not in the least.' The Queen smiled. 'Indeed, he dismissed the allegations at first – until he was told that they had been found in possession of the crown. He then said that Señor de la Garza would be taken back to Spain and tried there.' She sighed. 'I forbade it. Their father was English, therefore I claimed the right to punish them as my subjects. The two brothers are where they belong – locked in the Tower.'

I could not help but shiver at the thought of where the Jewel Master was now housed. I knew he would not be there for long – stealing the Crown Jewels is a most serious crime.

But something had been puzzling me. 'I do not understand how Tobias Bennett came to be Jewel Master,' I said. 'And where he got the name from. I thought the position was handed down in families, or only went to those who could be trusted.'

'You have hit upon the nub of the matter,' said the Queen, nodding. 'There is a story to be told. Our captive has been singing like a bird since last night, and now we know the whole of it. A Mr Tobias Bennett was due at the Tower ten years ago, travelling up from Portsmouth. He was from a family long associated with the Tower and the Jewel House – a nephew of the then Jewel Master. But the Master had not seen him since he was a child and, when a young man calling himself Mr Bennett arrived with all the right letters, he welcomed him into the family and taught him all he knew. Mr Bennett learned fast and proved himself a worthy successor to his "uncle".'

'But he was not the real nephew,' I exclaimed as the truth dawned. 'An impostor had taken his place!'

'Indeed,' said the Queen. 'Juan de la Garza – alias Hathaway – had just arrived in England, seeking revenge for the deaths of his father and sisters. He met the real Mr Bennett when they both sought lodgings at a Portsmouth inn and they became friends. But young Mr Bennett fell ill and died of a fever.'

The Queen shuddered. She has a horror of illness.

'Far from mourning his death, Juan de la Garza saw his opportunity,' she went on. 'He took the young man's papers and possessions. Now he pretended to be Tobias Bennett. He made his way up to London, joined the staff of the Jewel House and bided his time. He worked hard and was rewarded with the position of Jewel Master, and that suited his plan very well.'

She smiled at me. 'But you are my secret weapon against any who would work against me.' My heart soared at her praise. 'I know I can trust you with anything, my dear god-daughter, and may need to call on your skill again.'

I went down on my knee. 'I am honoured to be at your command, Your Majesty.'

She pulled me to my feet. 'Enough of this seriousness,' she said briskly. 'I am celebrating the anniversary of my coronation and I would dance! Let us send for the musicians.'

We made our way back to the Great Hall and the Queen's demands were swiftly met. Soon Mr Hatton was leading her in a Volta.

I managed to avoid any would-be partners and went in search of Ellie. I wanted to hear what she had thought of the display and to tell her what I had learned. But as I made my way through the crowds, I saw Daniel Cheshire. He had Lady Sarah by the hand and was leading her away from the noise. She looked reluctant – and a touch haughty. I followed. After all, I had kept his secret, so surely I had the right to listen in now.

Out in the passage he led her to an alcove and went down on one knee in front of her. Lady Sarah's face brightened at once at his pose. I took shelter in a doorway so that I could still see them.

'My dear love,' he began. 'Now at last I can tell you why I have been absent so often from your side.' I saw Sarah's face fill with dread. 'I have travelled to see your father, and mine, for a very special reason. And today, I swear, I have spent long hours trying to perfect the words to say to you.'

I could swear to that too!

He gazed into Sarah's eyes. 'Each hour that I

spend away from you is torture,' he said, 'yet a second of your company heals all my wounds. I love you more than life itself.'

This was sounding very fine, and colour was returning to Sarah's cheeks. Thank goodness he had not thought to propose in one of his dreadful poems. He went on to tell Sarah how she brightened his life like the very sun. It was simple and lovely. It was the sort of proposal I would like to receive — not that I will ever be silly enough to marry, of course.

Gazing earnestly at her, Daniel finished his speech. 'I beg of you to make me the happiest man in England, and consent to be my wife.'

'Oh, my love . . .' Lady Sarah spoke in a whisper and I had to crane forward to hear. I could see tears shining in her eyes. 'Yes, yes, yes,' she exclaimed. Then she looked worried. 'But what of the Queen?'

Mr Cheshire got to his feet and took her in his arms. 'We have her blessing!' he declared, swinging her off her feet. 'And that of our families. Now let us go to her and make it official.'

Sarah was pink-cheeked as they hurried back to the Great Hall. I stepped back into the shadows, but I do not think they would have seen me even if I had had a candle on my head. They had eyes only for each other. I quickly followed, and at the end of the dance I saw them approach the Queen. I was filled with amazement. She rarely gives consent to one of her close women marrying without throwing a few shoes!

Her Majesty called for silence. 'Among our celebrations, we also witness the betrothal of my dear Maid of Honour, Lady Sarah Bartelmy, and my loyal Gentleman of the Guard, Mr Daniel Cheshire,' she announced. 'May they know long years of happiness.'

Sarah glowed and looked very beautiful and Mr Cheshire stood proud. They made a lovely couple. I am sure I heard Mrs Champernowne sniff and get out her handkerchief. I glanced over to see how Jane was taking the announcement. Luckily she had a rather handsome gentleman fawning on her. I had a feeling she would not mind Sarah's news – for the time being, anyway. Then, at a signal from the Queen, a man who looked strangely familiar came forward with a small box, which he gave to Daniel. Now I could see that it contained the family betrothal ring, which he slid onto Sarah's finger. They were truly hand-fasted, with no less a witness than the Queen herself.

I suddenly realized that the man who'd brought the ring had been in the chapel with Daniel the day before. That completed another mystery. All strangers accounted for.

Alas, there is still one more thing and it is rather disturbing. With all the excitement and joy, I had forgotten about the theft of my daybooke! I still have no idea who took it. It cannot have been Mr Bennett. He would have seen me among Her Majesty's party when he was caught with the crown (and with Ellie) — he could have exposed me then. But he did not.

I looked around the Great Hall. Was the thief one of these happy, laughing faces? I searched for secrets in the eyes of those around me, feeling a thrill of dread every time anyone looked at me, and then engaged in private conversation. Was one of them the thief, telling his friend what he had found out about the Queen's god-daughter? Was my secret even now being passed from one mouth to another? I reminded myself that my daybooke had been returned to me — and surely no one at Court would believe the thief's tale without proof. Lady Grace Cavendish, running around the palaces of England, bringing thieves and murderers to justice? 'How ludicrous!' they would surely say.

Someone at Court knows the truth, though – and I can't rest until I find that person . . . or at least figure out what they hoped to gain by stealing my daybooke.

But for now I am well content to think of all that has happened in the space of one day. I have pleased the Queen by recovering her crown, and I glow when I think of the trust she puts in me. My dear friend Ellie has been present at the coronation celebrations, as she so deserved to be; Masou would get quiet recognition for his help and Lady Sarah is set for a happy life with her Daniel.

As I sit here beside the Queen's roaring fire, I know I can count on one thing. Life for Her Majesty's Lady Pursuivant will never be dull!

Glossary

Almain – a stately sixteenth-century dance

amulet – a small object worn around the neck, often as a charm against evil

Bedlam – the major asylum for the insane in London during Elizabethan times – the name came from Bethlem Hospital

bodice – the top part of a woman's dress

Chair of State – a ceremonial chair for a monarch

clothes press – a chest, closet or wardrobe where clothes are stored

coney – rabbit

daybooke – a book in which you would record your sins each day so that you could pray about them. The idea of keeping a diary or journal grew out of this. Grace is using hers as a journal

doublet – a close-fitting padded jacket worn by men

farthingale – a bell- or barrel-shaped petticoat held out with hoops of whalebone

Galliard – a sixteenth-century dance

Glass Gallery – a gallery exhibiting glass art

hand-fasted – archaic term for 'betrothal'

harbinger – somebody who went ahead to announce the monarch

hobbledehoy – an adolescent

hose – tight-fitting cloth trousers worn by men

Keeper of the Great Wardrobe – a position in the Royal Household, the Keeper was responsible for an office providing clothing and textiles to the Royal Family. The position was abolished in 1782.

kirtle – the skirt section of an Elizabethan dress

Lady-in-Waiting – one of the ladies who helped to look after the Queen and kept her company

laudanum – an opium tincture in alcohol used to aid sleep

Maid of Honour – a younger girl who helped to look after the Queen like a Lady-in-Waiting

marchpane – marzipan

Mary Shelton – one of Queen Elizabeth's Maids of Honour (a Maid of Honour of this name really did exist; see below). Most Maids of Honour were not officially 'ladies' (like Lady Grace) but they had to be born of gentry

mazed – perplexed, stupefied, confused

mummer/mumming – actor/acting

partlet – a very fine embroidered false top, which covered just the shoulders and the upper chest

Pavane – a slow and stately dance

penner – a small leather case which would attach to a belt. It was used for holding quills, ink, knife and any other equipment needed for writing

pike – a shafted weapon with a pointed head

posset – a hot drink made from sweetened and spiced milk curdled with ale or wine

Presence Chamber – the room where Queen Elizabeth received people

Privy Chamber – the room where the Queen would receive people in private

pursuivant – one who pursues someone else

Queen's Guard – these were more commonly known as the Gentlemen Pensioners – young noblemen who guarded the Queen from physical attacks

sarsenet – a fine, soft fabric often made of silk

Secretary Cecil – William Cecil, an administrator for the Queen (was later made Lord Burghley)

Shaitan – the Islamic word for Satan, though it means a trickster and a liar rather than the ultimate evil

small beer – weak beer

stomacher – a heavily embroidered or jewelled piece for the centre front of a bodice

tiring woman – a woman who helped a lady to dress

tumbler – acrobat

vellum – fine parchment made from animal skin

Volta – a sixteenth-century dance very popular with Queen Elizabeth I

woodwild – crazy, mad

THE FACT BEHIND THE FICTION

In 1485 Queen Elizabeth I's grandfather, Henry Tudor, won the battle of Bosworth Field against Richard III and took the throne of England. He was known as Henry VII. He had two sons, Arthur and Henry. Arthur died while still a boy, so when Henry VII died in 1509, Elizabeth's father came to the throne and England got an eighth king called Henry – the notorious one who had six wives.

Wife number one – Catherine of Aragon – gave Henry one daughter called Mary (who was brought up as a Catholic), but no living sons. To Henry VIII this was a disaster, because nobody believed a queen could ever govern England. He needed a male heir.

Henry wanted to divorce Catherine so he could marry his pregnant mistress, Anne Boleyn. The Pope, the head of the Catholic Church, wouldn't allow him to annul his marriage, so Henry broke with the Catholic Church and set up the Protestant Church of England – or the Episcopal Church, as it's known in the USA.

Wife number two – Anne Boleyn – gave Henry another daughter, Elizabeth (who was brought up as a Protestant). When Anne then miscarried a baby boy, Henry decided he'd better get somebody new, so he accused Anne of infidelity and had her executed.

Wife number three – Jane Seymour – gave Henry a son called Edward, and died of childbed fever a couple of weeks later.

Wife number four – Anne of Cleves – had no children. It was a diplomatic marriage and Henry didn't fancy her, so she agreed to a divorce (wouldn't you?).

Wife number five – Catherine Howard – had no children either. Like Anne Boleyn, she was accused of infidelity and executed.

Wife number six – Catherine Parr – also had no children. She did manage to outlive Henry, though, but only by the skin of her teeth. Nice guy, eh?

Henry VIII died in 1547, and in accordance with the rules of primogeniture (whereby the first-born son inherits from his father), the person who succeeded him was the boy Edward. He became Edward VI. He was strongly Protestant, but died young in 1553.

Next came Catherine of Aragon's daughter, Mary, who became Mary I, known as Bloody Mary. She was strongly Catholic, married Philip II of

Spain in a diplomatic match, but died childless five years later. She also burned a lot of Protestants for the good of their souls.

Finally, in 1558, Elizabeth came to the throne. She reigned until her death in 1603. She played the marriage game – that is, she kept a lot of important and influential men hanging on in hopes of marrying her – for a long time. At one time it looked as if she would marry her favourite, Robert Dudley, Earl of Leicester. She didn't though, and I think she probably never intended to get married – would you, if you'd had a dad like hers? So she never had any children.

She was an extraordinary and brilliant woman, and during her reign, England first started to become important as a world power. Sir Francis Drake sailed round the world – raiding the Spanish colonies of South America for loot as he went. And one of Elizabeth's favourite courtiers, Sir Walter Raleigh, tried to found the first English colony in North America – at the site of Roanoke in 1585. It failed, but the idea stuck.

The Spanish King Philip II tried to conquer England in 1588. He sent a huge fleet of 150 ships, known as the Invincible Armada, to do it. It failed miserably – defeated by Drake at the head of the

English fleet – and most of the ships were wrecked trying to sail home. There were many other great Elizabethans, too – including William Shakespeare and Christopher Marlowe.

After her death, Elizabeth was succeeded by James VI of Scotland, who became James I of England and Scotland. He was almost the last eligible person available! He was the son of Mary Queen of Scots, who was Elizabeth's cousin, via Henry VIII's sister.

His son was Charles I – the King who was beheaded after losing the English Civil War.

The stories about Lady Grace Cavendish are set in the years 1569–1571, when Elizabeth was in her mid thirties and still playing the marriage game for all she was worth. The Ladies-in-Waiting and Maids of Honour at her Court weren't servants – they were companions and friends, supplied from upper-class families. Not all of them were officially 'ladies' – only those with titled husbands or fathers; in fact, many of them were unmarried younger daughters sent to Court to find themselves a nice rich lord to marry.

All the Lady Grace Mysteries are invented, but some of the characters in the stories are real people

– Queen Elizabeth herself, of course, and Mrs Champernowne and Mary Shelton as well. There never was a Lady Grace Cavendish (as far as we know!) – but there were plenty of girls like her at Elizabeth's Court. The real Mary Shelton foolishly made fun of the Queen herself on one occasion – and got slapped in the face by Elizabeth for her trouble! But most of the time, the Queen seems to have been protective and kind to her Maids of Honour. She was very strict about boyfriends, though. There was one simple rule for boyfriends in those days: you couldn't have one. No boyfriends at all. You would get married to a person your parents chose for you and that was that. Of course, the girls often had other ideas!

Later on in her reign, the Queen had a full-scale secret service run by her great spymaster, Sir Francis Walsingham. His men, who hunted down priests and assassins, were called 'pursuivants'. There are also tantalizing hints that Elizabeth may have had her own personal sources of information – she certainly was very well informed, even when her counsellors tried to keep her in the dark. And who knows whom she might have recruited to find things out for her? There may even have been a Lady Grace Cavendish, after all!

A note on the Crown Jewels

The English Crown Jewels are famous throughout the world. They include priceless crowns, orbs, sceptres, rings and bracelets – all the regalia that is given to monarchs at their coronation. They have been used at the crowning of English kings and queens since Edward the Confessor in 1042.

When Elizabeth I was crowned in 1559, it was Edward the Confessor's crown – the 'crown of St Edward' stolen in the story – that was placed on her head. She must have looked magnificent, for she also wore a gown made of gold and silver cloth. This was a sort of hand-me-down, as her sister Mary had worn it at her own coronation five years before. The dress had to be altered, as Elizabeth was slimmer than the pudgy Mary.

Four hundred years later, it was Elizabeth II's turn to be crowned. Unlike her namesake, she had a new gown – made for her by Norman Hartnell, the top designer of the time. It was made of white satin and encrusted with precious and semi-precious stones. Like all the other monarchs before her, she was crowned with the crown of St Edward. But it was not the same crown as the first Elizabeth had worn. During the English Civil War, in 1649, Oliver Cromwell ordered the execution of King Charles I, after which he took over the country. Under Cromwell's republican rule, the Crown Jewels were either sold or melted down to make money. When the English monarchy was restored in 1660, the new King – Charles II – had to have all the jewels made again.

For more than six centuries the Crown Jewels have been housed in the Tower of London, where today they receive nearly three million visitors a year. They have been on view there since the seventeenth century. But they were not always as secure and well-guarded as they are now.

In 1671 a man called Colonel Blood went to the Tower under the pretence of visiting the jewels with his son and a friend. But in fact he was planning to steal them. Blood hit the keeper over the head, snatched up one of the crowns, squashed it and hid it in his cloak. His son tried to saw the sceptre in half to make it easier to hide, while his friend stuffed the orb down his breeches! They were arrested but, to everyone's surprise, Charles II pardoned the thieves and gave Colonel Blood a position at Court! It seems he was amused by the colonel's cheek.

After this, the Crown Jewels were better guarded

– although, in 1815, that did not stop a madwoman seizing one of the crowns and damaging it before it was wrestled back. During the Second World War the jewels were taken to a secret location to avoid the Blitz – and no one has ever revealed where that location was. The jewels are certainly very valuable, encrusted with rubies, emeralds, sapphires and pearls. The imperial state crown alone is set with 2,868 diamonds.

It was not always thieves that threatened the jewels. It was possibly also careless kings. It has always been said that, in 1216, King John lost some of the Crown Jewels in The Wash (a river estuary on the east coast of England, not a launderette!). John was escaping from the French, trying to cross the river with horses and carts while the tide was out. But the water came rushing back and the precious jewels were swept away. No one knows if the story is true, but it's an exciting thought that one day someone with a metal detector might come across the old Crown Jewels of England.